DEATH'S EMBRACE

JANEAL FALOR

OTHER BOOKS BY JANEAL FALOR:

Death's Queen
Death's Queen (Death's Queen #1)
Death's Betrayal (Death's Queen #2)
Death's Embrace (Death's Queen #3)
Death's Assassin (Death's Queen #4)

Mine Series
Mine to Tarnish (Mine Prequel)
You Are Mine (Mine #1)
Mine to Spell (Mine #2)
Mine to Fear (Mine #3)
Sacrifice of Mine (Mine #4)

Darkening Light
Ever Darkening (Darkening Light #1)
Savage Light (Darkening Light #2)

Elven Princess
Bound by Birthright (Elven Princess #1)
Bound to Endure (Elven Princess #2)
Bound by Love (Elven Princess #3)

Standalone

Goddess Ascending

A Genie's Heart

To Erik
For loving me always

CHAPTER 1

"A COUPLE CLAIMING to be your parents is here to see you." The servant waits calmly, belying what I feel at his words.

"What did you say?" I'm shocked out of my thoughts. It can't have been what I think he said.

"Two people who say they are your parents are here to see you. They have been waiting a rather long time and are quite persistent. I've checked for weapons, and they have none."

I sit back in the chair in the sitting room that's been mine for the past few weeks ever since Ranen entered my old room through a secret tunnel. We never did find the tunnel. This new room is made up to my taste. Simple clean lines, comfortable furnishings, a carpet, and a little more space so my ladies-in-waiting don't have to squish in as much when we meet in here. And space for sparring with Nash, if we ever get the chance again. Not that anyone else knows about that.

My mind switches back to what the servant said. It's hard to comprehend. There's no way they are my parents. Is there? I'm tempted to have him tell the couple that they should return when I'm holding an audience in the throne room, but I'm not sure I want the entire court and anyone else to hear this, Instead, I say,

"Send them to me. And tell Nash Zorris he's wanted as well." Because I don't want to do this alone.

With a bow, the servant leaves. I drum my fingers on my thigh, wondering if this is why Inkga suggested I wear a dress she designed today. She seems to have a sixth sense about these things. She would have me look my best to meet this couple, whoever they are.

My parents.

Can it really be?

No. Daros said I had no parents, leading me to believe they had died. Then again, it wouldn't be the first time he lied to me.

I jump to my feet and pace. The two windows show the grounds below and part of the lake. I'm on the second story now, at my insistence because it is safer. No more men crashing through the window. Though they could still come up, it'll be harder for them to do so. Plus, it's easier for me to get on the roof at night if I want, though I haven't done so in a while.

The clock on the wall chimes, but I don't pay attention to the hour. I avoid the low table that holds the treats the cook likes to send up whenever I have guests. I never partake, but my company seems to enjoy them. Well, once they get over the fact that I'm not eating with them. There's also a discreet door in one corner that leads to my bedroom. It's much like this room, though with a bed, dresser, and vanity instead of chairs.

The servant returns. "They're here, Your Majesty. Shillian and Carver Nilmac."

My chest constricts. "And Nash?"

"On his way, Your Ladyship."

"They can wait until after he arrives. I would like to speak with him first."

After he exits the room, I continue pacing. I put a hand on each of the daggers at my waist to make certain they're still here. It's not like they could go anywhere, but their presence gives me a certain reassurance. There are more on me, but I don't bother checking them.

I glance at the clock. What is taking Nash so long? He used to always be here when I needed him, but more and more, I'm waiting on him. He's changed since his kidnapping, but I don't want to say anything because of what he went through. Things might be different if I reinstated him as my Head Advisor, but I wanted to give him time to readjust after being tortured by Ranen and Daros's men.

That sick feeling I get every time I think of those men pummels me—Ranen because I killed him when I promised myself never to kill again, and Daros because he's still out there, hunting me. Both because of what they did to Nash. I shove the thoughts aside. The sick feeling eases but doesn't depart.

Where is he? It's been fifteen minutes.

I'm about to ask the servant for an update when there's a knock at the door. "Come in."

Nash enters. My heart skips a beat, like it always does when I see him. The man I care about is here.

The man I love.

His hair has grown out some—though it's still short—and his bruises have faded. But he's gaunt, and there's something disturbing in the way he won't meet my eyes. Despite that, he's all muscle. He exercises and practices his swordplay more than ever. From the thin sheen of sweat on his forehead, that's probably where he was. Hopefully, he's not too upset at my interrupting.

"You needed me?" he asks.

My heart gives a painful squeeze. I want to go to him and kiss away the pain in his gaze, but I stay rooted to my spot. "There are some people here saying they are my parents."

His eyebrows rise. "I thought they passed away."

"So did I. Either these two are trying to get close to me because I'm the queen, or Daros lied."

"You haven't talked to them yet?"

"I waited for you, if you don't mind sitting in on the conversation."

His response takes a moment. "Since Jem's your Head Advisor, you should probably ask her."

"I'd prefer if you were here."

His mouth twitches, but he doesn't smile. He never smiles anymore. "I'll stay."

"Thank you."

I take a seat in my usual cushy chair, and he tells the servant to show them in before sitting on my right.

The servant knocks, enters, bows, and says, "Presenting Shillian and Carver Nilmac."

Nilmac. Is that my last name? I pinch my fingers together, then unclench them when I realize what I'm doing.

The man I assume is Carver walks in, tall and gangly, with cold blue eyes, a rounded face, and long arms and fingers. He's wearing brown pants and boots with a cream-colored shirt and walks in with an air that says he's the one who belongs on the throne instead of me. His gaze jumps all over the room.

Following after him is the woman, Shillian. She has dark brown hair, blue eyes, and a long face. She's pale, except her cheeks, which are heavy on the rouge. She's wearing a white blouse and a red skirt that makes me want to cringe because of its bloody color.

They both bow and curtsy.

"Your Majesty, thank you for agreeing to see us." The man's voice is deep but scratchy.

I motion for them to rise. "I understand you think you are my parents."

"We are, Your Highness," he says.

The woman remains silent behind him, but her gaze is rattling, though I can't place why.

"You are mistaken. I have no parents." They unnerve me,

making me vacillate between wanting them not to have arrived here and wishing they'd shown up sooner.

"I know it's hard to believe since Daros was practically a parent to you, but I assure you it's true."

The fact that he knows I was raised by Daros doesn't mean he's my father. Almost everyone in the country knows that by now. I'm the Shadow Wraith, bringer of death, raised by the man who eludes me even now. Why did I agree to see them? "I'm afraid I see no validity to your claim," I say.

"I assure you it's true. You are our little girl," he says.

I grip the hilt of the dagger on my right hip.

I'm no one's little girl.

The woman steps forward like she can no longer contain herself. "You have a mole on your right foot, between your big and second toe."

I swallow past the thickening in my throat. I do indeed have such a mole.

"You used to cry until I sang you a lullaby," she continues. She sings a few lines of a vaguely familiar song before continuing. "You were such a beautiful baby. A joy I wanted for so long. When you came to us, I didn't think I could ever be happier. We named you Keera—bright star."

I work to keep my breathing even as I clench my jaw. This can't be. "If you were my parents, you would never have given me to Daros."

She drops her gaze and takes a step back as if my words sliced into her.

Carver says, "That's my fault."

"Explain yourself." I will my body to relax when all it wants is to be tense.

And yet...

"You see, when you were a baby, the famine was in full force, almaca disease raging. I worked to support our little family, but it

5

wasn't enough. I admit that I turned to a source I shouldn't have. I started gambling. Unfortunately, my debts ran higher than I could even imagine. Daros promised to take care of the debts in exchange for our only child. He had so much more than we did. You have to understand we were struggling to feed you, let alone ourselves. He could give you what we couldn't. Not just food, but also a life."

This would explain how Daros got a hold of me. Doesn't mean I believe it. "Didn't you wonder what kind of life he planned for me?"

"We assumed he was being a generous soul."

I snort.

Despite my disbelief that they thought giving me to Daros was for the best, their words ring true. And Shillian knew about my mole.

"Why wait all these years to come to me? Why not before? I was in one place the whole time. You could have visited."

"Daros said we couldn't," Carver says. "Though we tried once. We were turned away. We didn't think you desired to see us."

"But I would now?"

Shillian's voice is strong. "It was worth a try."

I don't trust any of it. I want to, desperately. "I will think on this matter. You are excused for now."

Nash stands and opens the door. "Please see that Mr. and Mrs. Nilmac have a place to stay for the night," he tells the servant.

They head out of the room, but at the doorway, Shillian stops and faces me. "I love you. I thought giving you up would be the best thing for you." She turns and goes.

She turns and goes.

My heart is shattered in a million pieces, already trying to put themselves back together.

I think I just met my parents.

CHAPTER 2

AFTER THEY'RE GONE, Nash returns to his seat. His presence is near enough to make me want more.

Shoving away my need for him, I ask, "What do you think?"

His response is slow in coming as he stares at his hands. "It's difficult to say. Do you have that mole?"

It would be so much easier if I didn't. "I do."

"They certainly know specific details about you, then. They may be telling the truth." He looks at me. "How do you feel about them possibly being your parents?"

My first reaction is to redirect the conversation away from my feelings. But this is Nash. I'm trying to do better at communicating with him. "I don't know. Mixed. Torn. I want a family so bad, but to think they gave me to Daros..." I shudder.

"It's unfathomable."

More than that—it's revolting. But I also know I didn't flash into existence. "This has me thinking... If they're not my parents, someone had to be. Someone gave me to Daros. Unless they died. But then, how did Daros find me?"

He shakes his head. "I wish I had answers for you." He takes my hand.

I ease back into my chair as his warmth travels up my arm. "We don't do this enough." My words are soft.

"I know."

I keep my voice low. "But it's dangerous." I keep quiet and pull my hand away.

"I know that too."

My eyes burn. I turn away. "Would you please send for Jem and Wilric?"

"Anything you wish."

He leaves to do so, but when he returns, we fall into an awkward silence. His words are sweet, but we both know they can never be. What I wish is for us to be together. I want to say something. More than that, I want to go to him—to comfort him and myself—but others are coming, and to be caught would mean his death.

His hand shakes as he runs it through his hair.

"What are you thinking?" I still whisper.

"Oh. Sorry. Nothing." He clasps his hands together in his lap.

"Are you sure it's nothing? You can talk to me." I hold myself back, hoping he does.

He looks down, and his words come out slow. Stuttered. "I—I was thinking back to… when I was being tortured."

When he says nothing more, I ask, "Do you want to talk about it?"

He takes a second. "I get nightmares."

"I used to as well."

"What stopped them?"

How do I answer? Do I tell him about the First Queen? Will he think I'm crazy? I trust him more than anyone else. There's a thought heavy on my mind that makes me not want to speak of her. But Nash is telling me things. Letting me in. I promised to do the same for him after he first came back to me. I open my mouth to speak when there's a knock.

Nash closes his eyes as if in pain before getting up to answer.

He glances back at me, expression clear of any of the torment he must be feeling. I nod, and he opens the door. Wilric and Jem enter the room.

"You called for us?" Wilric asks.

"Yes. I have a problem that needs delicate and thorough attention." I clear my throat. "If you didn't know, a couple claiming to be... my mother and father came forward."

Jem gives Wilric a sidelong glance before saying, "I heard rumors."

"I did, too," he says.

"They barely left. The servants put them up in one of the rooms with a set of guards. I'm tasking you both to find out if they are or not whom they say. Feel free to ask them or anyone else anything. It's imperative that I know if they are telling the truth, and if they are, whether I can trust them." I'd rather send Nash, but he doesn't seem to be in a good enough state of mind for such a task. Besides, I like him close. If I had it my way, he'd always be within sight, so I'd know no one had captured him again.

"You can count on us," Wilric says.

"I'll do whatever I can to help," Jem adds.

"That will be all, Wilric."

He gives a nod and leaves us.

"I wanted to speak with you about another matter, Jem. I highly value your view point and the help that you've given me these past several weeks, but I believe it's time that Nash regained his position as Head Advisor." It should be good for him. Give him something to focus his efforts on. And his opinion was always valuable. It will be good for the country, too.

Her expression reveals nothing of her feelings. "I was honored to serve you in that capacity as long as I have."

It wasn't much time, but I learned a lot about her. "I truly appreciate the job you did."

"Thank you, Your Majesty." She gives a curtsy.

"And you can continue on as a lady-in-waiting."

"I look forward to it." Her expression remains impassive.

It's just as well. As much as I want to know what she's thinking, it's better to be guarded from the world.

She give her goodbyes and is out the door.

Nash turns to me. "You didn't have to do that."

"Are you ready for it?"

"I am, but still, you didn't have to replace Jem. She's doing a great job."

"She is, but I want you back in that capacity, if that's all right."

"Very well, then." His expression changes. Softens. He reaches for a lock of my hair. "It's getting long."

"Yours is, too."

"Yes, but yours is growing fast."

"Maybe I should cut it."

"If you want." He runs his fingers through it.

I want to close my eyes and lean into him, but thoughts of Daros stop me. He always had me keep my hair short. Said it'd get in the way of fighting if I had it long. If I needed long hair to attract male attention for a job he made me wear a wig. It was a bigger hassle.

I should cut it. But I like it long. Nash is correct; it has grown faster than ever. It's almost to my shoulders. Usually I keep it up, so it's not noticeable, but today Inkga left it down.

I finally give in and lean into Nash's hand. It feels so good to let him caress me, even if we have to be cautious about it. After a minute, I pull away. "Would you make certain my council meeting is still on for today?"

"Of course." And just like that, he shuts off again, face closing up.

I shouldn't have pulled away. Should have stayed longer. But I always worry about being caught. About risking his life.

About wanting things I can never have.

CHAPTER 3

THE COUNCIL ROOM IS FULL. Jem is on my right, Nash behind me, and everyone else is in their usual places in the circle—those considered of highest importance closest to me. I would place them differently, but the positions were set up long before I was around.

I glance back at Nash.

His hands are shaking.

I'm not sure I should go through with this.

But he insisted he was well enough. I need to do this. "Thank you all for meeting with me today," I tell the council. "I want everyone to know I appreciate the job Jem Surah has done as my Head Advisor, but it is time for her to go back to being a lady-in-waiting. Therefore, Nash Zorris will return as my Head Advisor."

No one says anything, though a few look disgruntled. I suspect they would argue with me on this if they thought it would do any good. Then again, maybe they don't consider it worth fighting over when they can expend their energy on a topic they consider more important. I don't know. There's not enough I understand about my council.

Jem and Nash switch places. Having him closer is reassuring, and the shake in his hands is less pronounced. I doubt he'll ever be the man he was again, but I do hope he can regain at least some of his former confidence. I suppose it will take time.

"That brings me to the other purpose of our meeting today." I should have done this a long time ago. "I am changing a few laws, starting with those that call for the death penalty. I want no one to be executed for not paying taxes. If taxes cannot be paid, we will have the taxpayer work off their debt."

"It goes without saying that this is a brilliant idea, but I'll say it anyway," Yuka, Head of Arts, says.

"I disagree." Timit's voice of dissent is not unexpected, but it's unwelcome nevertheless. "If we don't have a strong enough incentive for country to pay their taxes, it will never get done. We won't be able to keep the government working."

"But with this plan, we will be able to employ those people as workers, instead of using their money for the job," I say.

"I think it's a win-win all around," says Mina, Head of Foreign Relations. "But I do worry that we won't get the skills we need to complete certain tasks."

"Those can to be paid with taxes, and we'll fill in the holes with the skills of those who can't pay their taxes." I sound more confident than I feel.

"You said, *laws*, Your Majesty. What other laws were you speaking of?" Monkia, Inkga's mother and Head of Staff, says. In truth, I like her daughter more than I like her, but perhaps that's because I don't know Monkia better. I may need to spend more time getting to know my council as people, and not only as a group that sits around this table.

"Several need to be changed." I take a deep breath. One I'd like to change is queens being executed if proven senile, but that takes the entire council to approve of, and I have more pressing needs. "Taxes will now be paid in livestock and harvests as well as gold."

"But how will we buy things?" Timit asks.

"We will still receive gold from those who can spare it, but we will use the produce to feed the country and the staff here at the palace or guards and government officials around the country. What we don't eat, we can give to the needy. The food could even be sold. There are all sorts of possibilities." I glance at Timit. "But I wasn't done. I'm also changing the law that says taxes are to be paid weekly. This is far too often, and besides, hard on our tax collectors. I propose we gather them once a quarter."

"Then people will find a way to cheat us," Timit says.

I want to roll my eyes but refrain.

"They won't cheat us," Sidle, Head of Military, says. "Not if the tax collectors do their job correctly."

I give him a small nod of appreciation.

"It would be a good way for us to stock up," Nidon, Head of Food, says. "Both getting paid with harvest and only acquiring funds once a quarter. Plus, it would save us money on not having so many tax collectors employed at an overworked cost."

"That is one of the things I was hoping for." I try not to show my relief that I'm getting so much positive feedback. It's not what I expected.

They continue to argue the merits for it, with only a few negative comments. I may have done something right for once. After everyone has had their say, I add, "Thank you for your support. Let's see that this is changed today and a decree is sent out to all of Valcora." While they're in a good mood, I might as well ask, "Another law I'd like you to consider changing, is the queen not being able to touch anyone."

Several gasps sound and someone hisses.

"Not happening," Timit says. "That is a long placed law with the purpose of keeping the monarchy moving through the Mortum Tura only. If a queen were to have a child, it could throw the whole government into chaos."

"I have to agree," Monkia says. "We can't have that type of distraction for the queen or the threat of repeating natural disasters should the country not follow the guidelines like has happened in the past."

As others continue to chime in against it, I want to pout but don't allow it.

Jaku stays oddly silent. What are his thoughts one the matter? I wish I knew. Would he be in support of Nash and me or not. It doesn't matter none of it is going to happen. I should have never chanced bringing it up.

Once they've gotten enough words in that sting to my core, I say, "Thank you for your time and your work on this matter. Everyone is dismissed, except Jaku and Nash. I need to speak with you both."

The council leaves with bows and curtsies but not looking me in the eyes. Only Nash and Jaku remaining behind. What is Nash thinking? Is he upset with me for asking or has he wanted to do the same thing? It doesn't matter. It's nothing that will ever change.

Jaku comes to stand beside Nash, hands at his sides. "You wanted to speak with us?"

It's such a relief to not have everyone *Your Majesty* and *Your Highness* and *my lady*-ing me all the time. Hopefully it's a trend that will continue, at least in more informal times, like this. "Yes. I would like to go out through Indell tomorrow, and I thought you'd both want to know and possibly even join me."

"Are you certain it's safe?" Jaku asks, as always caring about my life above everything else. It's as it should be, but sometimes it gets tiresome.

I keep my gaze on him, but watch Nash out of the corner of my eye. "No, but it's been a while since I've been out, and I'd like to see how my people are faring."

"I thought your ladies-in-waiting kept you appraised of such things."

"They do, and they're doing a splendid job of it, but it's not the same as going out myself. I'd like to. I'll go in disguise, but we can't be certain they won't recognize me, especially since I'll be going dressed as a guard."

"Whatever for?" The strictness of Nash's tone catches my attention.

"We need to warn them about Daros. We've sent word, but I want to make certain that precautions are taken. He's a dangerous person, and we've had no sign of him. I wish to make certain they know they need to keep an eye out for him. Make sure they know they can come to me." I'm proud of myself that my voice doesn't quiver in the slightest. Though my fear of Daros seems to be on the decrease after weeks having passed without us seeing or hearing anything about him, it's still there, hovering. Terror waiting to snatch me up. Or maybe I'm growing out of it. I'd like to think it's the latter, but the former seems more likely.

"We can do that. There's no reason for you to join us," Jaku says.

"Always trying to protect me," I reply. "You do a good job of it, but this is something I want to do. I need to warn everyone."

"It might be best if you went out as yourself instead of a guard, then," Nash says, surprising me.

"Do you think so? I know they are disgruntled over my flip-flopping the taxes around so much."

"I agree," Jaku puts in. "Is it worth putting the queen's life in such danger?"

Nash leans back in his chair. "The people will respect her more if she comes out as herself, instead of going in hiding—and possibly getting caught. Plus, I think they'll take it more seriously if she does it, and not a guard, like it has been done in the past."

"Why not meet some of them in the throne room, then?" Jaku asks. "We'd be able to control the situation much easier in those circumstances than if you went out into the streets."

I think about it a moment. "Control, maybe. But I think—I believe—that they will listen to me more if I go to them rather than making them come to me."

"You're willing to risk your life for a belief?" Jaku's face is tense. Stern.

"I am. Between my skills and the skills of the guards, I think it will be safe enough."

"Fine." The word snaps out of Jaku like a carrot breaking in half. "I will make sure you have plenty of guards, though."

"Not so many that the population is scared," I say.

"Would it make you feel better if some went out dressed as Poruah and Medi?" he asks.

"It would."

"Then it's settled," Nash says. "We're going into the town tomorrow."

He looks confident, but then, why do I hear a tremor in his tone?

I'm going out among my people because it's the right thing to do for them, but how will it affect Nash? Is this a good step for him, or too much too soon? I'm not certain of the correct answer. I want him back as he was, which will never be.

How much more will he have to go through, before he can come to terms with what happened to him? The torture, beatings, losing a finger. Maybe never. I'm still coming to terms with what happened to me. I can't expect more from him.

Nash and Jaku accompany me to the guards waiting at the door and then leave me. It's typical of Jaku to not stay around, but Nash used to come with me almost everywhere. Is he going out to practice more? Is he pushing himself too hard?

There's no time to think of it as up ahead I see the woman claiming to be my mother waiting in the hall. I'm not in the mood for dealing with more possible-parent problems.

She curtsies when I approach, and I motion for her to walk with me.

"Thank you, Ryn. I mean, Your Majesty," she says.

"Is there something you wished to speak to me about?"

"Yes. I wanted to know if there was something useful I could do around the palace."

I barely keep my step from faltering. "You want to help?"

"Of course. I'm your mother. That's what we do."

This remains to be seen. "It would be a good thing if you can stay in your rooms until I get a few things figured out."

"You mean until you know whether or not we tell the truth. I know you need to give the matter some thought, but is there some way I can assist with that? Something I can do to prove myself and your father?"

Why do the walls feel like they are caving in on me? "I appreciate you're trying to help, but I have many matters I need to attend to. It would be for the best if you talked to my lady-in-waiting, Jem. She will know what you can do."

"So you're not going to believe me until you have someone else check our story?"

I quicken my pace. "Where is your husband?"

"He's sleeping. I'm afraid he had a rough night and day and needed to relax a little before dinner."

"But you didn't?"

She purses her lips, as if pondering what to say. "I find myself wanting to be with you as much as possible rather than resting."

That thought stirs something inside me. Whether or not she's truly my mother, others don't usually desire to spend time with me. Unless they're looking for me to lead them. Maybe that's all she wants from me as well, but the child in me wishes it to be more. I squelch that desire. "I will see you later."

She halts and gives a quick curtsy. "Yes, Your Majesty." Then she hurries off, hopefully to her room.

I scamper to my own room, closing the door on my servant and guards and leaning against it. I rub my forehead. Too many things on my plate and not enough wisdom on my part to know how to deal with them.

CHAPTER 4

"SO YOU HAVE A FAMILY AFTER ALL," the First Queen says.

Perhaps.

"You are wise to look into them, but I'm fairly certain they're your parents."

I plop into a sitting position, ignoring the look she gives me that says I'm not using my manners. "How can you be sure?" I ask.

"They knew about your mole. But more than that, there's something about the way they look and feel that's familiar. Especially Shillian."

"You think she's my mother?"

"I do."

I can't trust it until Jem and Wilric return with confirmation.

"You've been through so much. I don't blame you, but maybe have a little faith."

"You think I should trust them, then?"

She hesitates.

"So I'm right to be cautious."

"Perhaps. I distrust them partly because you do, and partly because we know nothing about them. Being cautious is worth considering."

Before she can bring up anything else, I say, "What do you think of the law changes?"

Her presence seems to swell, becoming bigger than ever, though her actual size stays the same. "You are becoming a ruler."

And yet it has been a rough path, with too many things getting in the way of my caring for the country.

"You have had a difficult journey since becoming queen. I don't think you should be so hard on yourself. Relax. Let me take over." *Her words are soothing.*

I take a deep breath and let it out in one giant whoosh. "What would you have me do?"

She smiles. "I'm always here to help, even with your life."

"How can I do that? You're just here, in my mind. In my dreams."

"And yet you've felt my presence at other times, when you've needed me."

"I have."

"Then let me guide you."

After Daros, it's hard to have anyone guiding me, but she's nothing like him. "I'll try."

"That's all I ask."

* * *

I WAKE REFRESHED. Excited for the day. The First Queen may have faith in others, but I withhold judgment. Besides, today I get to go outside the palace walls. That, in and of itself, is reason for celebration.

After jumping out of bed, I put on a pair of black pants and a cream top. There are lots of belts for weapons, but the day is hot enough I won't be able to wear my cloak without suspicion. Instead, I hide my daggers inside my pockets and in my knee-high boots—safe enough to go out in public, but not so I'll frighten anyone.

I pull the rope that lets Inkga know I'm ready for her. This room came equipped with one. It's not something I usually use, but I'm anxious to get started today.

I move over to the dark walnut vanity and brush my hair. It's lighter than before. Almost as if I've been spending time in the sun, and not the night, roaming the roof and exercising. My eyes are bright, and my cheeks have some color. I look like myself, but not. Like a different person has taken a hold of me. And I suppose it's true. I'm not the quavering girl I once was. Even with Daros still out there, I'm fearing him less in the weeks that have passed with no sign of him.

It's the longest I've gone without him controlling me. Apparently, it's reflecting well on me. If only it would last. I flick a finger at my reflection. I shouldn't be so negative. It's hard not to give into what I've been my entire life, though. Today, though, I'm going to make a difference. I'm going to look my people in the eye as their queen, not Shadow Wraith, and tell them the truth about Daros.

I square my shoulders. Today, I'm giving myself and my city power over my fears.

It's not much longer before there's a knock on my door and Inkga enters.

"Morning, Ryn. You're up early this morning." She has a bigger grin than usual.

It's so nice to have someone use my name like I asked. "I wanted to get an early start. What are you so excited about?"

She comes behind me, takes the brush from me, and does amazing things with my hair. "Nothing more than you going out today. You've been wanting to go for a while."

"How did you figure that out? I haven't said anything."

"You didn't need to. You've been restless." She pins up my hair and weaves a thin crown into it.

"I admit I am looking forward to it." I think about Shillian and Carver. "Do you know if there's any news from Jem or Wilric?"

"There isn't. And before you ask—yes, I know about the two who say they are your parents. What do you think?"

I pinch my fingers together, then hurrying to relax them. I shrug. "I suppose I will know more when Jem and Wilric return."

"I hope they bring good tidings. You deserve some of that and more people who care about you as more than the queen."

Like her. She does a great job of caring about me, regardless of who I am now and despite what I've done in the past. How does she do that? Why does she care? I'm not brave enough to question her about it. At least not now when the morning is so bright. "I can't be sure they aren't here only because I'm the queen."

"Did you ask them about it?" She pulls up the last lock of hair and pins it in place. The result is a simple but elegant hairstyle that will stay in place all day.

"You're a genius with hair, among other things." When did I get so praise-y? I turn so I can look at her, instead of through the mirror. I give her the reason they gave me for not coming to visit sooner. "But it doesn't mean anything. They might still just want an in with the queen, whether or not they're my parents."

She sighs. "I wish life had taught you better than to be cynical."

Me too.

"What else do you need from me this morning?" she asks. "Should I call up breakfast?"

"Sorry. You'll have to eat without me today. I can't eat a bite." Is it because of excitement of going out and spending the day with Nash and those in Indell, or worry over my so called parents? Either way, food is not on the agenda.

"If you're sure." She moves to make the bed.

I feel guilty, having her do so, but she gets mad when I do it. Says I'm going to put her out of a job. I can't have one of my very few friends not be around anymore, so I let her have her way. "Positive."

I almost ask her why she stays around me, but I stop myself. What if it's only because it's her job? Besides, this morning I'm focusing on Daros. His capture—if not by me, then by anyone else. He can't hide forever if he's going to stay in my country.

After giving my goodbyes, I make my way out into the sitting room, and then the hall. Guards line the corridor, dressed in their steel plates, black capes, pants, and high boots. Jaku is among them. Nash is not.

"I thought you'd be here for an early start," Jaku says. "I've got guards undercover as people out in the crowds today. Probably the only people out and about this early. Are these enough to join you as the royal guard?"

Too many. "They should do. Where's Nash?"

Jaku shrugs, looking casual, but his eyes tighten with what looks like worry. "I haven't seen him this morning."

My gut wrenches. For a moment, I'm back to the day he was taken. Before that, he was always ready before I was. I steady myself. He's likely still in bed. Ever since he was brought back, he's been sleeping in as much. I thought it was because he wasn't my Head Advisor, and he felt awkward being around, but now he's resumed his duties, I can't be certain.

"Very well." I almost say we'll go without him, but I can't bring myself to. I want him near, not just because I enjoy being with me, but also because of his skills and his discerning thoughts. "We'll go fetch him, then."

Jaku nods. The guards fall in order around me as we head out. Those around me are familiar, even if I don't know all of their names. Julina, Eldim, Afet, and Jaku, I know by name. Wilric is absent, hopefully on the errand I sent him on and not out as one of the guards in the crowd.

We make our way through the palace, taking the shortest path possible to get to the barracks. The way is silent. I'm lonely, despite being surrounded by others. I'm grateful it's early, and we don't pass anyone in the halls.

Especially Shillian and Carver.

The grounds outside have a little more action. Guards are sparing, practicing, and patrolling. There are more now than ever before. Jaku insist, after Nash was found and Ranen almost killed him. He seems to think my life and the lives of those around me are in danger all the time. Then again, maybe that's how Jaku got his position. And maybe that's why Daros hasn't been able to kidnap another person close to me. Ranen may have been the main culprit behind the last kidnapping, but Daros was there and knew hurting someone close to me worked. It wouldn't surprise me if he tried it again.

Perhaps it's time to give Jaku a raise.

We head straight for the commander's barracks, where Nash lives. After he healed from his more serious injuries, he insisted in moving out of the palace and back to his old room. As we near, I hear a man scream.

I don't think. I run.

I shove my way past the guards, who must be too stunned to do anything? The fact that they aren't moving doesn't make me stop and think; it makes me move faster. Adrenaline makes my flight quick. My guards' footsteps thud after me, and Jaku calls me back, but I press on.

If that's Nash...

Someone could be hurting him again or trying to take him. I have to get to him. I have to save him from more harm. I rush through the open door, boots pounding on the wooden floor. The screaming gets louder.

I have a throwing dagger out, ready to use. With the other hand, I open the door to Nash's room. It slams against the wall.

My heart sinks past my feet. No one is attacking Nash. He's thrashing in bed, calling out in his sleep. I heave a sigh, wishing there was something I could do. He's having a nightmare.

"Nash," I call out, wishing I could wake him. With the others trailing in the room after me, it would be his death sentence if I touched him. "*Nash.*"

When he doesn't respond, I turn to the closest guard. Julina. "Wake him."

She doesn't speak, just acts. She's by his side in an instant, shaking him awake while softly calling his name. His eyes pop open, a glassiness to them, and his hand darts out and takes Julina by the neck. Afet jumps forward and tries to pry her free from Nash's grip.

My stomach roils. "It's all right, Nash. It's us. You were having a nightmare."

His face is white as he punches Afet in the face.

Afet darts back.

"Nash!" I scream at the top of my lungs.

Finally, he stops. The glaze over his eyes fades. His face grows paler as he lets go of Julina, who gasps for air and coughs. His voice is small. "I'm sorry. I didn't mean to."

She waves him away, even as she continues coughing.

Afet's gaze darts from me to Nash.

I kneel by Julina but make certain not to touch her. Not being able to touch anyone that's not assisting me with something important to my daily needs or my life is a pain. "Are you all right?"

She nods and chokes out, "Fine."

"Afet? You?" I ask.

"I'm good."

I glance at Nash, who's looking at the wall away from us. "Everyone out. Take care of Julina and Afet. Speak of this to no one."

"Your Majesty, I must insist on staying with you," Jaku says.

"He's awake. No one else is in here. I'll be fine."

He opens his mouth but closes it again and helps Julina out of the room. I shut the door after them and turn back to Nash. He's still looking away from me, the covers twisted around his legs. He's wearing a thin night shirt and pants. The fewest clothes I've seen him in. I knew he had muscles, but they're even more apparent without his armor on. My cheeks heat as my gaze flits over him.

I turn my gaze away, a quick look at his room. There's not

much here other than the bed, just a dresser with small knick-knacks carved out of wood. Did he make those? Or someone else?

"Nash?" I keep my voice soft.

"I don't want you here." His words are ragged.

I recoil.

He's hurting. How would I feel if I awoke to find myself choking a friend? Ashamed and embarrassed. Is that what he's feeling?

"It's all right. I'll leave. We heard screaming and came to see what was wrong," I say.

"I'm fine."

Clearly. "Are you still planning on going to town with us?" With me?

He lets out a great sigh, which moves his broad chest. I want to rest my head there. Give him comfort and whisper words of encouragement.

But I'm all too aware that he doesn't want me here.

"I need to change, and then I'll be out." His voice is hoarse.

"All right. I'll be outside." I ache to touch him, but after the way he treated Afet and Julina and the way he's acting now, I'm scared, too. Not that he'll hurt me, but that he'll reject me.

I give him one last glance—he's still staring at that stupid wall —and leave the room.

CHAPTER 5

A SHORT TIME later that feels like too long, Nash comes out in his soldier's garb. My heart skips a beat. He's so nice to look at. Unfortunately, my heart also gives a painful twist at the thought of what he's going through. The pain he must feel. The dark circles under his eyes. How long have they been there?

He won't even look at me. Or anyone else, for that matter. His gaze is somewhere off in the distance. Still, he comes to stand by me. That must mean something.

I hope.

We move together as a group, Jaku leading the way and everyone else surrounding me. I hope they don't expect us to stay this way the whole time we're out there. I'll never be able to talk to the people if I can't reach them. Yelling as a way to communicate doesn't seem like a good way to get things started.

We make our way through the open portcullis, and the guards keep it up after we leave in case we need to make a quick return, though many of them guard the entrance.

The air feels fresher out here than it does in the palace gardens. Cleaner. Freer. Yet there's a cloud hanging over Nash. I wish I could take his hand into mine, feel his skin, calm him, and help him like he's helped me.

Instead, I focus on going forward. On my people, who start to come into view. They stop and stare as we pass by. I want to talk to them, but I'll wait until the crowd gets larger. Still, I make myself smile. They simply stare back.

It's more crowded the closer we get to the market, but not as many as would be here later in the day. A few of them look familiar—they are guards out of their uniform. We don't need to talk to them; they know how dangerous Daros is. I only hope that's not because they're secretly working for him.

"Who do you want to speak with first?" Jaku asks.

I don't know where to start. At this point, those gathered in the market are staring at us even harder.

"Why don't we start with the shop owners?" Nash asks. "They will get word around well, especially if we buy something from them."

"Excellent idea." I'm grateful I thought to bring coins along. I walk to the nearest stall, and the guards around me clear a path, so I can look at the merchandise. They remain close, Nash and Jaku flanking me.

"Your Majesty," the male shopkeeper says with a bow. "How may I be of service to you today?"

How does he know I'm the queen? I figured everyone was staring because of our big group, not because I'm queen, but there has to be something. Ah—I'm wearing a tiara. Not my choice, but maybe it was a good idea. The city will see me for who I am and hopefully take my warning seriously.

I look over his wares—all sorts of candlesticks and candlestick holders.

The shopkeeper notices my attention and says, "We have the finest candles in all of Valcora."

Usually, when someone says that they're the best, they're far from it, but I take a candlestick that looks appealing. It's short, fat, and a cream color. "I'd like this, to use by my bedside at night. How much is it?"

"For you, it is free."

"I insist on paying. What is the cost?"

"It is an honor to serve the queen in any way I can. Please, take it."

I want to argue, but when he puts it like that, it's hard to counter. At least someone here seems to like me. "Thank you," I say.

"It is my pleasure. Would you like me to wrap it for you?"

"Please."

He takes the candle from me and wraps it in cloth, before handing it back to me.

"This is perfect." I don't know how to broach the subject I want to get into, so I jump right to it. "I was wondering if you could help me with something else."

"Whatever Your Majesty desires." He gives another little bow.

"There is a man—a very dangerous man—by the name of Daros Durkin. Are you familiar with him?"

The shopkeeper's gaze darts around. He clearly knows something but is uncomfortable.

"You can tell me. You don't have to be ashamed of whatever it is," I say.

He clears his throat. "Ah, right. I understand he is the one who outed you as the Shadow Wraith." His voice shakes on the last two words.

Maybe he's not giving me something out of respect, but out of fear. Not what I want. "Yes. He did do that." My voice is soft. I strengthen it. "He escaped our dungeons before."

"I had heard that."

"Have you heard how dangerous he is? That Daros will find a man's weakness and use it against him in any way he sees fit?"

The shopkeeper shakes his head.

"I want people to appreciate how very dangerous he is. We

need any news you hear of him reported, even if he threatens you. The crown will protect you." I show him a drawing I had done of Daros.

After looking at it, he puts his palms together and bows his head over them. "Forgive me for being so impertinent, Your Highness, but if you can't protect yourself and those close to you, how are you to protect anyone else?"

I wipe all expression from my face.

"Her Majesty has that power and more," Nash answers for me.

"Until Daros is apprehended and sentenced, we will place anyone with information in the palace, if they wish to stay there, as long as that information is accurate."

He bows again. He bows far too often. He says, "I will keep that in mind and spread the news to my customers."

"Thank you." I take my leave of his stall, hoping the rest of the shopkeepers we visit will not be so invasive.

The next stall holds cloth. Wool, from the looks of things. I should have brought my ladies-in-waiting. They would be the perfect addition to this group while shopping. No matter. They aren't here, so I'll have to do my best. I'm not sure I want to place them in extra danger, anyway. It's one thing to send them out with guards, but another to have them accompany me and the dangers that come with being by my side.

I run my fingers across some gray material. The market becomes more crowded, with people still staring at me. I pick up the gray piece of cloth and show it to the woman at the stall. "This is fine wool. It would make a wonderful cloak for use in the winter. How much?"

Her face is stern as she names a price far above what I know it costs and adds a *Your Majesty* that sounds almost sarcastic to the end of it.

Do I call her out on it or pay her? The assassin in me wants to call her out. Instead, I hand her the amount she asked for. She smirks and pockets the coins.

"I heard what you said to Derlyn. Is it true that Daros is dangerous?" she asks.

"He is. We're hoping to thwart the worst of the problems he could cause."

"Hmm."

I show her the image. "If you or any of your customers have news, they can pass it along to any guard or bring it to me personally. As I told Derlyn"—who I assume was the shopkeeper I just spoke with—"we will do everything in our power to keep them safe."

"I'll pass on the word." Though she sounds like she'd rather hammer a nail in her own foot.

I wonder if she'll spread the word. If any of them will.

I continue talking to shopkeepers and show them the image— some more enthused than others, especially when I buy something from them. I end up purchasing a bag to store all my purchases. It will hamper a fight, if there's to be one, but I can drop it.

If Indell—the capital of Valcora—seems to have such negative opinions of me, I wonder what the rest of the country thinks.

We're finishing up at the last vendor, my bag heavy with items, when a young man who's all limbs comes up to my guards and requests to speak with me. I move closer, so there's only a guard between us. "Can I help you?"

"Yes, Your Majesty," he says with a bow. "I thought you would want to know that I think I spotted Daros."

My heart gives a little flop. "What did this man look like? When did you spot him?"

"It's been some time." He looks down, rubbing the toe of his foot against ground. "Last week. He was wearing a brown cloak. He had thick eyebrows and dark eyes, and he was thinner than fashionable."

The *thinner* part doesn't sound right. I can't imagine him

anything other than rounded with fat and muscles. Still, I can't let this go without looking into it. "Where did you see him?"

"At the Red Lady Inn."

I glance at Jaku, who is already whispering to another guard, and he gives me a nod. I turn my attention back to the young man. "Thank you for your information on this. Would you like us to take you back to the palace to keep you safe?"

He shakes his head. "I'll be fine. I'm living with my brothers, who are burly. Besides, Daros looked like he was heading out of town."

"What makes you say that?"

"He had a large pack with him. Plus, the Red Lady Inn is on your way out of town."

Or he could be coming into town—if it even is him. "Thank you for your information." I hand him some coins, which he takes. "If you change your mind about staying at the palace, please let a servant know. I'll send word to be on the lookout for you."

"I will." He nods. "Thank you for being good to us and lowering taxes, Your Majesty."

When I got around to it, anyway. "You're welcome."

He leaves, and Jaku comes to my side. He says, "I've got my men on it."

"Please report their findings to me. Though I'm not certain it was him."

"The description was a little different than what I saw at your ball, but it's worth checking out."

I'm glad I'm not the only one who noticed. "Thank you for your work on this."

"It's my job. Now let's get you back to the palace. If Daros is running around Indell, we don't want to make you an easy target."

I want to protest, but he's probably right. Besides, my stomach is growling. I may have grown soft, being fed on a regular basis, but I like it.

As we head back to the palace, I wonder if more of my countrymen are going to be grateful I lowered taxes, like that man, even if I switched back and forth until I came to a final decision. Or they may be like some of the others we met today and not want to talk with me. Whether that's out of fear or disdain, I have a long way to go.

CHAPTER 6

THERE'S a knock on my sitting room door before a servant opens it and says, "Jem, Your Majesty."

"Show her in." I wiggle back in my chair and get comfortable.

A moment later, Jem walks in with two more servants who carry what looks like a painting accompanied by the man who is the painter. I have an inkling I don't want to see it.

Jem is expressionless as she says, "Are you ready for the unveiling of your portrait, Your Highness?"

It's what I was afraid of. "Certainly."

She motions to the servants, and they walk around until the image is facing me. It's part familiar, yet part unexpected. I'm on a throne, with a crown atop my short, dark hair. It's longer now, and it's held up by pins. In the picture, I'm sitting so straight it's like I've become a brick wall, only wispier. My head is held high, and there's a shine in my eyes.

The painter certainly portrayed me in a flattering light. "Thank you for your hard work."

He bows. "It was an honor to paint for Your Majesty."

"We'll make certain the country is aware of who painted the masterpiece," Jem says.

Not sure that I'd call it a masterpiece because of the subject matter, but I appreciate what Jem is trying to do.

Jem motions for the servants to leave with it, and the painter follows after them. She picks a seat across from me. "They are working on copying it and sending it throughout Valcora."

Joy. "Very well." It took some time to complete the painting, even after I was done sitting for it. Maybe it will take time for it to be passed to the citizens.

Jem daintily clears her throat. "I have news for you, concerning Shillian and Carver Nilmac."

Already? I lean forward. "What did you and Wilric find out?"

"Wilric would have come with me, but Jaku had an errand for him."

I wave her concern away. "What did you find?"

She studies me before saying, "As far as we can tell, they are upright citizens. It's true that Carver had some gambling problems, and that they were very poor during the famine." As was most of the country, from what I understand. Jem continues. "Several neighbors remember them having a little girl. They said one day she was just gone. When they questioned the parents about it, they said they gave her away to someone who could take care of her, keep her belly full, and prevent her from getting almaca."

I want to pace, but don't want to turn my back to her. "Do you believe they are my parents?"

"Yes." It comes out as a whisper.

My parents.

The tumult of emotions isn't something I'm prepared to deal with. They're a tangled mess, writhing inside me. I don't know what to do with them all.

How can this be? How can I believe it?

How can I not?

These aren't things I can ask anyone but myself.

There is a real question that needs asking, though. "Are they

connected to Daros in any way other than their giving me
to him?"

She shakes her head. "No. It appears Daros paid off Carver's
debts, and in exchange, they gave him their three-year-old daughter." Her voice holds the tiniest note of disgust.

I can't say I blame her. I'm thoroughly disgusted myself.
Wanting the best for a child they couldn't take care of themselves
is something I understand, but they should have checked what
type of person Daros was. How he was going to treat me.
Raise me.

In their defense, I don't think Daros ever raised a child before.
Or since.

But knife it all. Why did they have to give me to him? Why
couldn't they have kept me or given me to someone who wouldn't
raise me to be a monster?

I want to throw a dagger at the wall but don't want to lose my
temper in front of Jem, so I keep seated. Calm and collected.

Another thing catches my attention. She said I was three when
taken. *Three.* I wasn't given to Daros as a baby. I grew at least a
little with parents who hopefully loved me. Why can't I remember
any of this? Why are my only memories of childhood harsh and
unrelenting?

"And you think that child was me?" I ask.

"By all accounts, yes," she says.

Dagger it all, I can't believe it.

I have parents.

And they gave me to Daros for money.

My stomach rolls and lurches. I swallow the bile, hating the
acidic taste in my mouth. Hating it all. "How did they find out that
Daros would take me in?"

"I don't know. Wilric and I weren't able to find out."

Who knows, then? He came to them and offered a lump sum
in exchange for their child? I clench my teeth. I don't want to talk

about this anymore. "Thank you for your assistance in this matter. I trust you and Wilric will be tight-lipped about it."

"You have my assurance that we will be." She twists her hands together—a very uncharacteristic behavior for her.

Either she's lying, or another thing is making her nervous. "Is there something I can help you with?"

"Yes." She hesitates, dropping her hands to her side. "Would you teach me to fight?"

I would never expect this. I don't know what to say.

"I've shocked you." She sits demurely, hands finally holding still.

"I admit that. Why do you want to fight?"

"Because there are many dangers in court, not all of them barbed words."

I snort. She gives me a look that says I shouldn't be so unlady-like, but I ignore it. The idea has merit, though I've never trained anyone before, unless you count sparring with Nash. I can't touch her in order to train her—not without causing her death. As much as I trust Nash to keep our touching a secret, I don't trust Jem to do the same. She's very rule abiding, though it would mean her death if she did. Still, I'm not sure I want to risk either of it.

"We'll have to enlist help." Nash is the first who comes to mind, but I'm not sure he's the right person for this job. He trains hard as it is. Too hard. I don't want to give him another excuse to overextend himself. But there is someone else I trust. "What about Wilric?"

The corners of her mouth tug upward for the slightest moment. "He would work."

"Are you certain you want to do this? I won't go easy on you, and I won't allow Wilric to either."

Her fingers knot together. "It's needed."

And if there's anything Jem seems to like, it's doing what's needed. I, on the other hand, follow too many of my wants. "Would you like to go on a walk with me?" I ask.

"Certainly. The gardens?"

Perfect. I didn't even have to suggest it. "That would be nice."

Together, we make our way out into the hallway, where my guards join us. It's not what I want—we'll draw far too much attention to ourselves with an escort—but facing Jaku's wrath for not taking them isn't something I'm in the mood for. Besides, they'd probably ignore me if I told them to go away.

We're silent on the way to the gardens—the best place to talk, though that's not why I want to go.

When we step outside, Jem says, "The weather is lovely."

"Indeed, it is." Though that's not my reason for wanting to come here either, it's a nice side effect. There's a crispness to the air, but the sun shines through the fluffy pink clouds. There's a scent about, something like apples, almost. But more than that, it's the sound that makes me quicken my pace. The noise of blades, clashing together.

Is Nash out there?

Of course he is. He's so rarely elsewhere these days.

"Is there something you wished to discuss with me?" Jem asks, as we continue on to the gardens.

What can I say? I doubt she wants to talk about training when there are others around to hear. Fighting would be more interesting than any discussion subject I can think of. Before I make up my mind, those training come into view. I let my gaze flitter there and back. It's all I will allow, but it's enough to see Nash in full guard dress, sweat beading on his forehead as he blocks his opponent.

My throat tightens, my heart feeling as if it leapt out of my chest to join him.

"Your Highness?" Jem whispers.

Though I'm no longer looking at Nash, guilt slices through me. I shouldn't be so concerned over him when I've a country to run and Daros to look out for. Besides, I'll never be able to have him.

I clear my throat. "I thought a walk would be nice."

"It is." She comes to a halt, facing the soldiers in front of us.

There aren't words enough for the praise I want to heap on her for that action. It leaves me free to watch Nash unhindered by expectations. He's got a sheen of sweat across his forehead, his arm muscles rippling as he thrusts his sword forward toward his opponent. With his swift movements, I can't see his missing pinky, but I know it's gone. How has it changed his fighting?

Whatever the difference, he appears as much able to take care of himself as ever, if not more. He's rapidly wearing down his partner with maneuvers that send my heart pounding. I wish it was me up there against him. My body aches with repressed movements.

I realize I'm leaning forward and force myself to straighten like Jem is beside me. She doesn't hold my attention long, though. Nash fills my senses even from so far away. I remember the smell of him. The way he feels when he puts his arms around me. The taste of his kiss. And watching him fight is like an agonizing sort of joy.

Just seeing him is reassuring to my soul, but not being able to do more than look tears me to shreds. I have to focus on something else or I'm going to lose my tight control. I take a look at the man he's fighting. I believe it's a guard named Piru. He's been helpful in the past, and I'm grateful he's continuing to be so with Nash now.

Despite knowing I should keep control, my gaze flits back to Nash. He doesn't appear to have spotted me, which is for the best. Other guards keep glancing our way, but he keeps a firm grip on the fight.

It's just as well he doesn't notice me. My heart wishes otherwise, but it's really for the best. I force myself to turn away from the fight and say to Jem, "Shall we?"

"Let's. I'm looking forward to spending time in the garden."

We wander away, my back burning like someone is watching me, but it's probably just my wishing that Nash was focused on me after his fight was over. I turn my attention to Jem. "I'd like a way to get to know you personally a little better."

"What would you like to know?" There's the faintest note of surprise in her tone.

"What about your family? Tell me about them." I worry I made a mistake by asking. I've never heard any of the ladies-in-waiting speak of family, except when I first became queen and they offered to let my parents stay at the palace too.

Of course, I had no parents to speak of.

"I haven't seen them in about a month, but they write every week. Last I heard, they were doing well. It's hard to think of them when I feel so removed from them."

They're alive. I hold back a sigh of relief. "Is it the distance? Couldn't they come to the palace as well?"

"Only the queen's family joins her at the palace. Ladies-in-waiting aren't to be distracted by anything, from serving Her Majesty."

"That doesn't seem fair."

She shrugs. "Perhaps to you. It's so ingrained into me from childhood, I hardly think about it. It's a little odd how much you don't know about your country and customs."

"Because of how I grew up." It was nothing like her experience.

"I suppose so." She grows quiet.

"Tell me more about your family," I prompt.

"I'm an only child. Which might explain why they had a hard time letting me go, despite preparing me for it."

We reach the gardens, and my guards enter before us, as the sound of blades clashing grows faint. I want to stay and watch Nash, but I don't want to draw attention to him more than I already have.

She says, "Mother cried the entire way to the castle when they were dropping me off. It's been twelve years, but I remember the tears streaming down her face."

"What about your father? Was he sad to see you go?"

"I believe so, though he was always more reserved with his feelings. He never once cried, but his eyes were red when I last saw them that day. But he handed me a note, which I've kept. He wrote many things in it, but mostly about his love for me."

What would that be like—to have the love of parents I've known my whole life? It's hard enough, getting to know them now, let alone returning the love they claim to feel. "Are their letters like that, still? If it's not too personal to ask."

"I don't mind. The truth is I love talking about my parents, but I don't get an opportunity to do so very often. They're very supportive of me. I think they were grateful you drank the Mortum Tura and became queen instead of me. Not only did they fear I wouldn't live through it, they also knew the responsibilities would be heavy on my shoulders.

"I do know they prefer me as a lady-in-waiting, where I can be of influence and high in the government, but without so much pressure or death hanging over my head. They don't know how close I've come to seeing you die, though, or they'd have begged me to come back home."

"We did have that close call..." An attacker came crashing through the window, back when I wasn't sure I liked Jem. I'm still not entirely sure, but I definitely like her more than I did.

"And I wasn't far off when you fought Daros at the ball."

"You weren't?"

"Yes. I was nearby, until one of the guards saw me and hustled me away. Which is probably for the best, but another reason for"—she glances around—"what I asked you earlier."

"It would probably be for the best."

We continue to talk, but I'm stuck on how to teach her to fight. Nash would be a much better teacher, but maybe Wilric will be good too.

CHAPTER 7

LUNCH TIME, and I invited my parents.

My parents. Such a strange thought.

It's quiet and awkward at the table.

I've hardly touched my food. Instead, I glance around the small room. It's meant for informal luncheons, like this. We're seated at a round table with a turntable in the middle where the dishes are for us to serve ourselves. Light from three narrow windows brightens the room. I almost wish it were dark. Then I wouldn't have to look at anyone.

After how talkative they were before, I expected them to be the same now. Maybe my accepting them to a degree made them as unsure of what to say as it did me.

My parents look like they haven't been eating. They shovel in big spoonfuls, instead of dainty bites, and when they do speak, it's with their mouths full of food. I had no idea my time at the palace turned me into such a snob, but apparently it did. Or maybe I'm looking for something—anything—to focus on besides *them.*

It's only when I glance at them out of the corner of my eye that I catch them watching me.

"How are you enjoying your rooms?" I ask.

"They are wonderful," Shillian says. "I've never been in one like them before. Thank you for the accommodations."

"Certainly." On the chance of being rude, I must ask, "How long do you plan on using them for?"

She drops her gaze.

"We are at your mercy," Carver says. "You see, we would love to spend time with our daughter, but we know how busy you must be. We can only hope you will be comfortable with us staying awhile, but we will go whenever you're ready for us to. Don't feel shy about kicking us out."

I want to do that, and yet I would like to know them better. It's a mess. How is one supposed to act around parents that abandoned them? "What about your jobs?"

"I'm afraid I lost my job last month," Carver says.

That doesn't bode well. "And what was that?"

"I am a mason."

I nod. Maybe I can find work for him, and then he'd have no reason to stay. Or maybe I should use it as an excuse to keep them close. I don't know what I want. "A good profession, to be sure."

"It's hard work."

"But honest," Shillian says.

"And you, Shillian? Do you have a job?" I ask.

"I take in laundry when I can get some, but more and more of my clients are turning to other laundry ladies."

Why is that? I want to ask, but I've been rude enough as it is. "I'm sorry to hear that."

"It is what it is, Keera."

I bristle under the name. That's not who I am. "You will call me Ryn."

Her face turns the same color as her rouge. "Oh. Forgive me. I've called you Keera so long in my mind, it's hard to think of you with any other name."

"It's fine. I just prefer *Ryn*."

Is it wrong to choose a name of my liking instead of the one my parents gave me at birth? I don't know the right answer, but I'm Ryn. I have been for a while now, and I don't want that to change because the couple who didn't raise me gave me a different name.

The discussion lulls again. What are they thinking? Are they judging me for using *Ryn*? No matter. I'm not changing my mind.

I find myself wishing Nash or one of my ladies-in-waiting were here. They'd know what to say and how to get out of this awkward conversation. Or non-conversation. Why did I choose to dine with them again?

In an effort to break the silence, I ask, "What was I like as a child?"

Shillian beams. "You were precocious. You walked and talked early, always babbling about something. You seemed genuinely happy and rarely cried, even when we couldn't feed you enough."

That statement disturbs me. I wasn't upset about not having a full belly, but they still gave me away. Granted, I might have died, had they not given me away, but my heart doesn't want to listen to that.

I wait for her to say something more, but nothing comes. The air is heavy with unspoken words, and it's pressing on me. This isn't what I want to be doing, or where I want to be doing it. As much as I want to hear about my childhood, it hurts.

"If you will excuse me, I have to attend to my duties." I stand.

They rise as well, bow, and give thanks.

"I will see you later. Please feel free to enjoy the palace. Any of the servants can help you with whatever you may need."

"Will we see you again soon?" Shillian asks, a tender note in her voice that makes my heart quiver.

"When I can get away from my obligations." It's the best I can offer, for now.

I head out of the room, my usual entourage surrounding me. I'd like to be alone with my thoughts. Too many of them are crowding my head. I could burst through them and run away, like

I did after my first dinner as a queen. When Nash followed me and showed me back to my rooms. That would be much preferable to now.

Being alone with Nash... A tiny sigh escapes me. Luckily, no one seems to notice, or if they do, they don't say anything.

When I get back to my rooms, a male servant I'm unfamiliar with waits for me.

"I was told to deliver this to you, Your Majesty." He bows and hands me a note.

A hint of fear grips me at the thought of the notes I've received in the past, but I open it and read.

SLIPA ZORRIS IS HERE to see you. I have directed her to wait until you are ready. This servant can show her to the room you wish to see her in.
Faithfully yours,
Kada Pinoch
Head of Relations with the Queen

THE FEAR LEAVES me as several thoughts run through my head at once. Nash's mother? Here to see me? What does she want? Is it something to do with Nash's behavior? And what is Kada doing? She's never once before sent me a message like this. I suppose it's her job, but I didn't think she would care to be involved in such small details.

Maybe I finally won her over? Unless she has an ulterior motive.

"I would like to see Slipa Zorris in my sitting room, if you please," I say. "And send up a tea service for her."

"Yes, Your Majesty." The servant hurries off.

My mind is full of all sorts of comings and goings as I enter my sitting room. A guard already searched the space thoroughly and declared it attacker free.

I take my usual chair. What could Slipa want? Have I done something to upset her? Has Nash? Is she going to demand I release him from service and send him home? Would that be for the best? It's difficult to say whether having duties is better for him or not. He's been overworking himself either way.

After the tea service arrives, I don't have to wait long before there's a knock at my door and the servant introduces Slipa. She enters the room with grace. I have the strangest urge to run up and hug her. I don't dare, of course. I would never risk her life in such a manner. "Please, have a seat and something to eat," I say.

She picks a seat near mine and takes a slim biscuit. "Thank you for seeing me."

"It is an honor, I assure you. How are your daughters?"

"Good. Getting into a little more mischief than usual, but I suppose they're at the age for that." The concern in her gaze belies the calmness of her tone.

"Is something upsetting you?" Something I can assist with?

She fidgets with the cuff of her sleeve. "I wanted to know... I was wondering if..."

I make my voice soft, like Inkga taught me. "What can I help you with?"

Her eyes fill with tears. "Nash. He hasn't come home in weeks. He sends letters and money, but he hasn't been around at all. After his rescue, I thought we would see more of him, if anything, but he doesn't seem to want to be around us. I'm worried about him."

As am I. "I didn't realize he was skipping out on your visits."

She nods.

I tap my finger on my leg. "He is working hard around here. He practices hours a day, and I made him my Head Advisor again."

"He wrote that you had."

I wish I had something for her, but there's nothing. "I don't know how to help."

"I understand. I hoped..." She gets a far-off look in her eyes.

"Hoped what?"

"It was silly of me."

I put the tiniest amount of force in my voice. "Hoped what?"

She sighs. "I thought, with how much you seemed to care about him when he was taken, that you'd be able to do something for him."

Her logic doesn't make sense. "I'm afraid I'm having as hard a time as you are."

"What with?" Her eyebrows furrow.

I shouldn't have opened my mouth. Now I'll make her worry more. "He's a little different now. More focused on practicing fighting and less on helping with the government."

"I feared there was something, though I wasn't sure what. A mother knows these things."

The talk of mothers reminds me of my parental problems. If anyone can help me with them, that might be her. First, I need to soothe her concerns about Nash. I wish someone would soothe mine. "I will encourage him to make a visit home, but I'm not sure he'll listen to me."

"If he'll listen to anyone, it'll be you." For the first time since she entered the room, there's a light in her gaze. "He respects you, Your Majesty."

He has a funny way of showing it.

"I shouldn't take up any more of your time," she says, rising.

"Actually, I was hoping you could help me as well."

Her eyebrows rise a fraction as she sits back down. "I'm happy to assist however I can, Your Highness."

How do I tell her what my problem is? I don't know if I should, but I want advice from someone who knows what I'm talking about. "My parents have been found. They came forward a few days ago. The thing is I don't know what to do with them. They are strangers, and..." I try to think of a way to describe what I'm feeling, but it's hard. I'm not accustomed to sharing. "I don't know if I should trust them."

"That is a problem, indeed. Time will be good—give you a

chance to get used to the idea of having them. No matter what happens, know that family is in the heart, not the blood. Though you have nothing to lose by giving them a chance."

Do I have nothing to lose? Maybe she's right. I should try to get to know them. If they make their way into my heart, I can accept them. If not... Well, I'm sure I can find Carver a mason job in another city, far from here. "I appreciate your council," I say.

"Thank you for honoring me with your trust. I promise to keep it safe between us. Is there anything else I can assist you with, Your Majesty?"

"No. Your words were more than I hoped for. I'm glad you came today. I'll do what I can with Nash, though he has a mind of his own."

She gives a chuckle. "That he does."

We give our goodbyes, and she takes her leave. Is she right? Do I have nothing to lose? I fear I do. What if they leave again, like the woman who taught me to read?

I'll have to work past that fear, since they seem intent on staying.

CHAPTER 8

I WAKE from a dreamless sleep with only hints of the First Queen and hurry to get ready. Inkga helps, and we chat about her latest designs as she does my hair. After I'm done with breakfast, I dismiss her and think about my day.

My first priority is my country, then comes Nash, and then my parents. Since I have no meetings with the council or ladies-in-waiting until later, I can speak with Nash first. I send a servant for him and watch a couple of birds out my window.

While I wait, Jaku comes in.

"Any news of findings at the Red Lady Inn?" I ask.

"A few people spotted someone similar to who that young man described, but they don't know where he went after that. I'm not convinced it was Daros, but if it was, the trail went cold."

How are we ever going to find him? "Thank you for looking into this matter."

"We'll keep at it until we find him. I can promise you that."

I want the words to buoy me, but if Daros doesn't want to be found, he won't. Nothing will stop him from that.

Jaku excuses himself, and I focus back on Nash. He's a much

more pleasant subject than Daros. What is it that has me so nervous? Is it because I have to summon him? I hope they don't find him having a nightmare again. It can't have been easy for him to be seen in such a state of vulnerability. Not that I think him vulnerable, but if I was in his position, that's what would be going through my head.

A good half-hour later, he arrives to my sitting room.

"You wanted to see me?" He voice is oddly formal.

"Please, sit." I take a seat to encourage him to do the same. He doesn't sit as close as I'd like, but he's not far, either.

"I had a visit from your mother yesterday." I wanted to speak to him earlier, but there wasn't time with all I had to do. This is the first chance I had to speak with him.

He drops his gaze. "What did she need?"

"She's worried about you." When he doesn't respond, I fall to my knees in front of him so I can look into his lowered eyes. I grasp his fisted in his lap. "I'm worried about you."

He pulls away, stands, and moves to the window with his back to me. "There's no reason for concern."

I want to go to him. To wrap my arms around him. But he refused me once. I won't be put off again. "You're so different than before you were taken. It's to be expected that you'd have a hard time with things, but not that you'd push me or your family away. We want to help."

He whips around, his eyes a blaze of a tormented soul. "No one can help."

I struggle to keep my anger and sorrow down. "Don't you think I know what you're going through?"

"You do. Of course, you do." He runs a hand through his short hair. "I want to face this alone. Want to fix it myself."

"How is shutting out everyone around you going to fix it? Allow us to help."

He scoffs. "You're one to talk. You don't let anyone in."

"I let you in."

"No. You gave me a glimpse of what's inside of you—nothing more."

The words sting with truth. "I'm trying."

"And so am I."

I take a step closer. "Do you want to talk about it?"

"No."

"Maybe you should anyway."

"No."

"I thought we agreed a question asked for a question answered. That we would help each other along." I don't know what else to say at this point. If this doesn't work, I'm out of ideas.

He's quiet and turns away from me. "I have no questions for you."

"Well, make something up. I want answers from you. How are you sleeping?"

He whips around. "Look—I don't want to talk about it, all right?"

I try to ignore the bite. "We could spar, then. We haven't done that since you got back."

"What? So you can beat me? I think not." His words are bitter. Too bitter for him.

I clear my expression. "Then you can at least visit your family and do your job as my Head Advisor."

His face softens. "I didn't mean to hurt you."

"I'm not hurt." Much.

"You've closed yourself off. Of course, I hurt you." When I don't say anything, he continues. "I'm sorry I don't want to fight you. I'm not ready for it yet."

My heart melts a little. How much pain is he going through? It makes sense he doesn't want me to beat him. He doesn't want to feel helpless again. Useless. At least, that's what I guess. Maybe he has some other, unfathomable reason. "It's all right, but you should visit your family. They're worried."

"I know I should. But that I'm not ready to see them."

"Do you mind telling me why not?" I brace myself for rejection.

He sighs. "I don't want them to see how weak I am."

Oh, Nash. "You're anything but weak."

"I don't want to talk about it."

"All right, if that's what you want."

"It is."

What do I say, then? I take a seat, and he follows suit. I say, "What do you think about the laws I changed?"

"You did good. They needed to be made less harsh. You found a way to do so but still get what the government required."

His words warm me. He approves. I didn't even have to go to him for advice. I came up with it all by myself, but still I did a good job. "I feel like it's not enough. That I want to do more for my country. I just don't know what that is yet."

"You'll figure it out."

"With your help, perhaps."

He doesn't respond.

The silence is awkward. Uncomfortable.

There's a knock at the door. I've never been so grateful for an interruption when I'm with Nash.

He answers it, and a servant enters and bows.

"Your parents request an audience," the servant says to me.

I glance at the clock. Duties call. I've spent more time with Nash than I should have. "They'll have to wait. See if Kada can arrange a meeting time for them that won't clash with my schedule."

"Yes, Your Majesty."

The servant leaves, and Nash says, "I understand your ladies-in-waiting will be here soon."

Drat them. I'd rather spend more time with Nash. "It is their time. Yes."

"I'd better get going then." He moves to leave.

I stop him by grabbing his hand, the touch tingling my skin. "Nash."

He doesn't turn. "Yes?"

"Please visit your mother. I can give you the afternoon off for it, if you'd like."

"I'll see her on my day off." His answer is soft and will have to be enough.

"Thank you."

He gives my hand a squeeze, lets go, and is gone.

It's the squeeze that gives me hope things are going to be all right. But it's a small hope.

CHAPTER 9

THE GARDEN IS WARM—ALMOST too much—as I sit at a table outside with my parents, playing a game of nako.

"Thank you for spending time with us," Shillian says for the third time.

"It's no trouble." Mostly. "I'm sorry I have such a busy schedule."

"We understand. Don't we, dear?"

Carver looks up from the game he and I are playing. "What?"

"Oh, never mind." She looks at me conspiratorially. "He always gets like this when playing games. He's very competitive."

Carver moves a piece, and I one to counter him. "That's not always a bad thing."

"I suppose." She folds her hands primly into her lap.

While I wait for him to make another move, a new thought crosses my mind. "Do I have grandparents?"

She gives a sad smile. "You did. Carver's parents died in a fire when he was a teenager." Though he's sitting right there, she leans forward and whispers, "He doesn't talk about them much." After a quick glance at him, she sits back.

He moves his peg, saying nothing. I counter with one of my own and focus back on Shillian.

"My parents were a good sort. They were so excited when we finally got pregnant with you. My father was a wood carver, and he made you a cradle. Mother spent hours making you clothes and blankets from scraps she found. It was a trying time, but a happy one." Her eyes grow distant.

While I wait for her to continue, Carver and I switch several turns.

When her gaze clears again, I ask, "What happened to them?"

"Sorry, dearest. Though it's been years since it happened, I still miss them." She pulls out a lacy handkerchief and dabs at her eyes. "When you were born, they doted on you. Your grandfather would carve toys out of sticks, and your grandmother gave you everything she could. But the famine was not kind to them. They caught Almaca." Her voice breaks.

The only sound is birds chirping.

I want to ask her what happened, but I know. No one survives from Almaca. Why they were so driven to give me away makes more sense now, even if they made a poor choice in doing so.

Or maybe not so poor.

I'm here, after all. I didn't die of hunger or Almaca. I may have once lived a hard life, but now I'm surrounded by luxury. I have my health and friends. Skills and no more torture. If I didn't know better, I'd almost say I'm happy. If I continued to live with them, would that be the case? There's no way of knowing.

Carver moves his piece, and I skip a peg piece one.

"After they were gone, we felt so alone," she says. "They were good people and took good care of us. We loved them and missed them. That's when Carver fell into his gambling habit."

He stares at the nako board, chewing on a fingernail.

"But we're here with you now, and that's what matters." Shillian gives me a big grin.

"I'm grateful for that," I say.

Carver moves a piece, and the thrill of victory dims some of the longing for memories of my grandparents. That ache will always be there, though.

I move my final piece into its peg, trapping Carver's. "I won."

He scowls.

"He's not very good at winning, and neither is his attitude when he loses, I'm afraid," Shillian says.

I want to ask why he was so insistent that we play, then, but I'm working hard on not being rude. "That's all right."

"What would you like to do now?" she asks.

I'd rather go back to my room and talk to Inkga or Nash. Maybe have some alone time. There hasn't been much of that lately, and it sounds divine.

"I know," she says. "We can take a walk through the gardens. Isn't that a grand idea, dear?"

"What?" Carver says. "Oh, yes. A walk would be nice." But there's still a scowl on his face.

"Only if you want to." I almost hope he says *no*.

He cheers up. "Don't mind me. Shillian is right. I have a hard time losing. Let's go for a walk. It will clear my mind and give us a better chance to know our daughter."

We stand and stroll through the gardens, my guards following subtly. It's silent. Uncomfortably so. I don't know what to talk about. What would be good for us to discuss? It's hard to think about anything except being back in my room. And Nash.

"What was Daros like when you were growing up?" Shillian asks.

I consider telling her, but I'm sure she doesn't want to know. What parent would want to know their child was tortured, trained hard, and forced to kill? "He was probably like you'd expect."

She frowns, a line forming between her eyebrows. "We should never have left you with him."

No. They shouldn't have. "What's done is done."

"You're right. Now we can be a family again." She beams at me.

I force a smile, but I'm afraid it isn't very heartfelt. They're trying to impose a bond that needs time to be forged. I can't make myself love them instantly, as happy as that would make them.

CHAPTER 10

I SLEEP ONLY a little that night. I spend the day in council meetings, signing paperwork, then meeting with the people in the throne room, and after that, chatting with the ladies-in-waiting, I'm ready to call it a day. Unfortunately, Shillian is waiting at the door to my room.

"There you are, darling," she says when she spots me between my guards. "I have the best idea. Why don't we go shopping together? It'd be the perfect mother-daughter activity."

The market is still open this time of day. Blades and poisons. She is taking what little free time I have. I can still climb up to the roof tonight and spend some time wandering around up there, if she hasn't worn me out by then. "I need to check with my Head Guard. Why don't you come in while I send someone to fetch him?"

I don't need to check with him, but it may give me a reason to stay here.

We enter the sitting room. She babbles on about the market and how we'll be able to find clothes there, maybe even matching outfits. I school my expression to be neutral. I match nobody.

It feels like too long until Jaku comes, though it's only about ten minutes.

"You called for me, Your Majesty?" he asks.

"Yes. Shillian here would like to take me to the market, to do some shopping. I was wondering what you thought of that." I stare into his eyes, hoping he gets the hint that I want him to say *no*.

He's quiet for a moment. "We'd be able to swing it for you, if you go in disguise and take guards with you."

Ugh. No such luck. "What's the point of going in disguise if my guards come with me?"

"I'll have them change into Medi clothes. That should keep any attention away from you. In fact, I'll join you. I'm done with my duties for the day."

"You don't have to do that."

"It would be an honor to serve you." He gives a bow to me and a slighter one to Shillian. "If you'll excuse me, I'll go change and meet you back here with some guards."

"Thank you, Jaku." The tone of my voice says otherwise. I don't care.

Shillian is dressed for a trip to the market, in a plain brown skirt and maroon blouse. She has a matching handkerchief over her hair.

"Let me change into something less flamboyant. I'll be back momentarily." I leave before she has a chance to respond.

Back in my room, I move like I haven't a care in the world. There's no point rushing, except maybe to get this over with. As I pull on a black skirt, I think perhaps I shouldn't have such a bad attitude. Maybe I should invite Inkga or the ladies-in-waiting along. Then again, it would probably be best to go with just Shillian. We're going to have enough company with the soldiers.

I slip on a light blue blouse and a pair of black boots. It's easy to stash daggers on my person, and my poison pouch is at my neck. All is as it should be. I glance longingly at the bed. Its time will come.

Even going in disguise, I expect a few people—if not more—to recognize my face. Hopefully, that doesn't become too big a problem. I leave my hair as is, twisted into a bun and pinned to hold the short strands in place.

Nothing left to fiddle with, I return to my sitting room, where Shillian is looking out the window.

"I'm ready," I say.

"Wonderful." She turns with a smile on her face, though it doesn't quiet reach her eyes.

I wonder what that's about, but I'm not about to ask. "Where's Carver today?"

"He's playing cards with some of the off-duty soldiers. Seems they like having a new person to play games with, and Carver likes to play to relieve the stress of looking for a job."

"I hope he finds something soon."

"As do I."

I go out of the room. Jaku has returned with guards in casual garb. I must have dallied longer than I thought.

It takes some time, but we make our way out of the palace, through the open portcullis, and to the market. We're quite the spectacle—a group of us, shopping. I keep my head down, but we're not the only group out. There are many others. The market is bustling.

We glance at some of the stalls, but Shillian doesn't seem interested in them. Why did she drag me out here if she doesn't want to look? We come to the area where the stalls turn into shops, and she perks up. We glance at the windows of several but don't go in any. Maybe this will go more quickly than I thought.

Until she stops. "Ah, here we are," she says. "My favorite."

Lovely. A dress shop. And from the look of the windows, a girly one. Not at all my style, though it's Shillian's, apparently. I may not be related to her after all.

Julina steps forward. "I'll go in with you."

"The rest of us will wait out here." Jaku gestures with his finger, and they spread out so they're close enough to reach the shop quickly if needed, but not so they'd impede the way of the other shoppers.

Julina stays close to me, not caring that Shillian wanders farther toward a section of lace. She *oohs* and *ahhs* over it. I exchange a glance with Julina, and we both stifle grins. Neither of us is much for frills.

I turn my attention to the bolts of cloth. Despite the flounces of the shop, the material is nice. Maybe I could find something to turn into a dress—just not as overdone as the shop itself.

"You have a fine eye for nice things, Your Majesty." A woman walks up to me and curtsies. She's clear-eyed and smiling, showing a gap between her two front teeth. Her brown hair is up in an elaborate bun. She wears lacy and pink clothes, fitting the shop.

So much for my disguise. "Thank you."

"I would be happy to fashion something for you at no cost."

I glance at Julina, to see if she knows why the woman would do so. Julina shrugs, and I turn my attention back to the shop-keeper. "That's very kind of you. While I do like this cloth, I have someone at the palace who designs my clothes."

"I see." She purses her lips. "Maybe I can interest you in more materials then." She heads toward the back of the shop, where more bolts of cloth await.

Julina gives me another shrug, and I leave her to follow the woman. There are so many colors—bright and muted hues, as well as black and white.

"I think you'd look wonderful in this red." She holds up a length of cloth to me.

Blood flashes in my vision. My stomach churns. I gently push the fabric away, trying not to look at it. "Red isn't for me."

"All right, then. How about this nice blue?"

A crash sounds behind me.

I whip around, daggers in hand. Attackers are pouring in the shop. Men and women, all armed. Where are my guards? I hope they're not incapacitated. Julina keeps her back to me but moves closer, sword in hand. Together, we can put a big dent in their numbers.

A shrill cry pulls my attention to the middle of the shop on the right-hand side.

My mother.

I rush forward. I have to protect her. She'll never survive on her own. I rush forward. "Shillian, get behind me."

Julina is at my side in an instant, Shillian racing to get behind us. A man thrusts his sword at her but misses. I hug the side of the table as she squeezes past. "In the corner." There, we'll hopefully be able to hold our own until help arrives.

I shove bundles of cloth to the floor as we go. Footsteps tread after us, heavy on the wooden floor. I turn around and run backward, hoping I don't trip over anything. We make it to the nearest corner before the attackers get to us and manage to block Shillian in between Julina and me, a table full of cloth and Julina on my left and a wall on my right.

The attackers come at us from both sides. I have to trust Julina to help keep Shillian safe.

Unless she was the one that told them we'd be here.

I cross my daggers in time to block a sword aiming for my chest. "Why are you attacking us?"

The woman with the sword sneers at me and presses closer and closer. I move, giving her room, before thrusting my arm back out and up. She slams her blade down, but it's too late. My dagger cuts into her with sickening familiarity.

I pull back, bringing my weapon with me, slick with crimson.

The woman falls back, and a burly man takes her place, leaving me little time to think. Our blades clash together, the sound of metal hitting metal clanking through the air. Sweat beads on my forehead. Behind me, Shillian whimpers. I look to make certain no one has gotten through Julina's barrier. Shillian is safe.

I am not.

A sharp blade slices into my thigh, just above my knee. I hiss, moving my blades in a flash of silver and red. The man's expression of glee quickly transforms to something more like fear. Within moments, I've dealt him three wounds. Not one is serious, but he backs up and moves aside for another to take his place.

"How many of you are there?" I growl.

"Enough to kill you," my new female opponent says.

"Did Daros send you?" I ask.

"Wouldn't you like to know?" She thrusts her sword forward.

I dodge and restrain the urge to throw my dagger. A quick glance shows me the room is teaming with attackers ready to take her place. I need to keep as many weapons as I can until things get desperate.

Things feel pretty desperate now.

Where are my guards?

I go back and forth with the latest attacker, trading blows with her with ease. I sneak a peek at Julina out of the corner of my eye. She's holding her own, but I don't know how long she can last. I know how much I've been training and practicing at night; I have no idea how much she does.

As I spar with my attacker, a movement closer than I'd like catches my eye. A couple of assailants are walking on the table to get to us. They'll have easy access to Shillian if I'm not careful. I send my blade flying. It flies into my current attacker's shoulder.

The two on the table aim their blades down at me. I block with the dagger that's out, but without a second one, it takes more strength and maneuvering. A blade comes at me from the front. I block it, only to have the attackers from the table come at me. They're going to get to me before I can move.

Out of nowhere, Julina swipes them away with her sword, pulling their attention on her. My attacker is small enough that I can see another man waiting behind her to get to me. He grins wickedly, but I force my attention back on the problem at hand.

There's a loud ruckus at the front of the store. I look between the legs of those fighting us on the table to see the rest of my guards barreling in. My relief is palpable. No matter my skill level, I can only take on so many attackers.

The woman fighting me comes on harder at the sight of my guards.

"Give up. They're going to take you out," I say between breaths.

"I'll do my job first."

"What's in it for you? Give up, and maybe things won't be so bad."

For the briefest moment, she hesitates.

That's all I need.

I whack her sword away, twisting it out of her hands. She raises her arms in surrender. It's not long before the rest of the uninjured attackers in the room do the same.

The shopkeeper comes out from under a table. I didn't realize she crawled down there. "What have you done to my livelihood?" she asks the attackers.

Shreds of cloth are strewn around the shop, bolts everywhere. It's a splattered mess of color. "Rest assured the crown will pay for the damage done."

The shopkeeper sniffs. "Thank you."

Who will deal with all these criminals, though? My guards will love this task.

"Are you well, Your Majesty?" Jaku asks.

"Fine." Though blood is seeping down my leg.

"We need to get you back to the palace."

"Yes, let's get you safe," Shillian says.

I wait to answer as I look around the room again. About a dozen attackers are kneeling or laying on the floor, weapons on the ground. "We need to take care of these people first."

"My guards will see to that."

"I'm sure they will." I grab hold of the shirt of the girl in front of me and pull her close, pressing my blade to her belly. "Who are you, and why did you attack me?"

"If I tell you, will you let me go?" her voice quivers.

"Don't tell her nothin'," the man behind her spits out.

I ignore him. "I can't let you go, but your sentence will be minimized."

Her gaze darts around the room, and then back to me. "We were hired."

I let her take a step back, easing my dagger from her stomach. "All of you?"

She nods.

Someone either knows me well or wants me gone. "Hired by who? Daros?"

She licks her lips.

"The opportunity to lessen your sentence is going out the window."

Her hands tangle in one another.

"Tick tock." I need her to talk.

"It was a group of Kurah."

Not Daros. My shoulders relax, though it may be worse that a group of Kurah want me dead and have enough money to hire attackers to do the deed. No. Nothing is worse than Daros.

The Kurah make sense. Sort of. They have enough reason to be angry with me over raising their taxes, and money they could pool together can afford to hire this many assassins, though they didn't fight like they were trained. Perhaps just thugs off the streets who needed the money. Whatever the case may be, I've made myself some rich enemies, with power and connections. Unless Daros is one of those connections. He may not involved in this after all.

Another thought comes at me with such force my stomach

revolts. I turn on Shillian. "Did you lead me here? Did you know the attackers were going to come here?"

"How could you think such a thing? I just wanted to spend time with you." Her wide eyes fill with tears.

"Begging your pardon, Your Majesty," says the attacker who explained the Kurah situation to me.

"What is it?"

"She had nothing to do with it. We've been watching the palace, waiting for an opportunity to strike once you were out of its fortifications."

The oomph goes out of me. "You will be taken well care of if you speak the truth."

She lowers her head. "I'm sorry I attacked you. It's only that my family needs the money."

"What for?"

"I have seven siblings that aren't getting enough to eat. I had to find some way to feed them."

A knot I didn't know was in my stomach loosens. "We'll feed them, but you have to understand I can't let this action go unpunished."

She bows her head. "I understand."

"And I need to know who the actual Kurah is that sent you."

"I don't know. I never actually me—"

The man behind her darts forward, his sword angled toward me. "You will die."

The woman I was talking to stabs her blade backward, slicing into him before he can reach me. Another second, and Jaku is shoving the man backward, although the wound to his stomach is likely lethal.

"You will not harm the queen," Jaku shouts. He ties the man's wrists before turning him over and pressing a cloth to his wound.

I glance back at the short woman. "You saved my life."

Her gaze drops.

When she says nothing, I tell her, "This will be taken into

account when your punishment is decided." I lean closer without touching her. "Thank you." If she hadn't joined the fight, this could have all turned out different, despite her joining to kill me. Her motives were noble, even if her methods were not.

As one of the guards takes her, I turn back to Shillian, whose cheeks are wet with tears. I sigh. Being a daughter is much harder than I expected. "I'm sorry I accused you of leading me into a trap."

"That's all right," she says, but still doesn't look at me.

I lower my voice. "I've been taught to fear everyone my whole life. To see plots everywhere I go. I'm sorry I took it out on you."

She licks her lips. "Not your whole life. There was a time we took good care of you. And we will do our best to do so now."

Warmth stirs in my chest. I clench my jaw to keep my emotions in check. It means more to me than I can say.

CHAPTER 11

I ENTER my sitting room with a large stick as a walking support and find Nash. I want to rush to him, but Shillian is still with us. "Nash," I say.

"I heard there was an attack." His fists are balled up.

"There was, but everything is fine. Not much damage was done."

"Not much?" He glances me over and notices the gash in my dress that shows a piece of cloth tied around my thigh. He growls. "I should have been there."

Normally, I'd agree, but with the state he's been in lately, I'm not sure that would have gone over well. "It's all right. Just a scratch."

He tightens his jaw. "Let me at least call for a healer."

"One is on the way." I sit in one of my less used chairs, putting the walking stick to the side. If I'm going to bleed, I don't want to do it on my favorite.

He brings another chair over for me to put my leg up on. I hold back a wince as I prop it up.

"You should have seen her in action," Shillian says. "She was like lightning, acting with a brutal but quick strike."

Nash nods, not taking his gaze from me. "I know. I've seen her."

A blush floods my cheeks. I glance down to cover it.

A servant enters and says, "The healer is here to see you."

The healer rushes in the room before the man's done speaking. She says, "Where's the injury?"

"It's not bad. Just on my thigh." I motion to the affliction that's tied up below my skirt. With permission from the shopkeeper, I tore a length of cloth off one of her bolts and tied it around my wound after talking with the girl who saved my life.

"Let me have a look at it." Her voice is calmer now, though still stern. She looks at Nash. "You should leave."

He clenches his jaw. "I'm her Head Advisor. I have a right to know how she's doing."

"Yes, and we will inform you, but for now, you need to exit the room."

Before he can protest further, I say, "It's fine, Nash. I'll send word."

His face tightens, and I think he wants to argue more, but he leaves the room without another word.

"You should be cautious with that one," the healer says, barely above a whisper.

"What do you mean?"

Her gaze drifts to Shillian. "If you will permit me, Your Majesty. I need to check the damage."

"Of course." I lift my skirt to just above where I tied the cloth that's now red with my blood but at least not soaked.

She uses deft fingers to untie the knot and release the cloth from around my leg. She prods at the wound. "It's not too deep, but it'll still need stitches."

"She's going to be all right?" Worry colors Shillian's words.

"She's going to be fine." The healer doesn't say anything about infection, but hopefully, we can ward that off before it's an issue.

Shillian's shoulders fall as if the tension goes out of them. "Praise the sun."

I'm grateful, but not surprised. I'm more worried about Nash, his reaction, and the healer's words about him. "Shillian?"

"Yes, dearest?"

"Would you inform those waiting outside of my prognosis? Let them know I'll be fine. I'm getting stitches, and then I'll rest."

"I can do that. Do you want me to come back afterward?"

I try not to wince at the raw hope in her gaze. "No, thank you. It'd be best if I were alone to sleep."

"What about dinner?"

"I'll send Inkga for something from the kitchens."

"If you're sure..."

"Yes. Thank you. Your help is appreciated." And her getting away from me long enough to let me think even more so.

"All right. I'll see you in the morning."

I give her a smile that I hope looks sincere. "We'll talk then."

As soon as the door closes behind her, I turn back to the healer. "What did you mean about being cautious with Nash?"

She studies me carefully, looking deep into my eyes. "If you will forgive me, Your Majesty, that your preference for him is obvious."

"I don't know what you mean."

"I believe you do, though you attempt to underplay it. I understand why. This is dangerous territory. Everyone can see how you feel about him, though you try to hide it. You made it even more clear when he was taken and you fought so hard to get him back. I don't know how long the council will leave him be, though you haven't touched."

At least nobody knows we've touched. Still, her comments make me want to never even look at Nash again if it's going to get him in trouble. "I'll take your words under advisement."

"If you care about him, you will."

She pulls supplies out of her bag, but my thoughts stay on our conversation. What am I going to do? How am I going to do accomplish ignoring him when he's my Head Advisor? I need to keep things professional.

I'll have to figure out a way because I won't risk his life.

CHAPTER 12

THE COUNCIL MEMBERS are crowding my sitting room, while my leg is resting on a chair. Last night, I went to sleep worrying about Nash. When the First Queen appeared, I refused to talk it over with her, instead discussing politics.

Now it's time for a meeting, but the healer said I needed to stay off my feet. Rather than making servants carry me all over the palace, it'd be easier to have the council come here. None of their advisors will fit in the room, so it's only the main council and me.

Nash is on my right, his presence burning that side of my body.

And through it all, I can't even look at him.

I force my thoughts to the council members settling around the room. It's been a trying twenty-four hours. I'm not sure I'm up for this. Doesn't matter. I'll do it anyway.

Keeping my expression neutral, I watch the rest of them sit in order. "Thank you for coming to my sitting room today. I know it's an inconvenience. What's on the agenda today?"

"We should discuss what took place yesterday," Jaku says.

Not what I want to rehash, but at least it's nothing to do with

Nash. "By all accounts, the attack was sent from the Kurah. They are upset over their tax situation."

"Which is why we should lower their taxes," Timit says.

Not that I'm surprised, but for once with him, I'd like to be. "You're only saying that because you are one of them. Besides, giving into them because they sent attackers after me is not a good precedent."

"You did set the precedent when you gave into your Head Advisor's kidnappers." Timit looks smug.

The rest of the room is silent. Out of the corner of my eye, I see Nash make a tight fist. I keep tension out of my body, like I haven't a care in the world. I manage to refrain from pinching my fingers together. "I may have done so at first, to get him back, like I would hope any of you would want, but as you may recall, I decided against it in the end. We need to take a firm position that we won't give into such threats."

"Even when your life is in danger?" Sidle, Head of the Military, asks.

"Even then." I sound as confident as I am. "But the question remains—what are we going to do about it?"

"I say we install a flat tax. One that will be fair to all." Timit beams at his own suggestion.

"A flat tax is not fair to all. It casts the heaviest burden on the Poruah and the least of it on the Kurah." I did pay attention in all those lectures I got when I first became queen.

"I agree with the Queen," Mina, Head of Foreign Relations, says.

"I think we can all mostly agree on that, but what else can we do?" Kada asks.

When the silence becomes uncomfortable, I say, "I propose that we use the money we have stored in the treasury to ease some of the burden. From what I understand, we have plenty in there." I have yet to see it for myself—something I should remedy.

"We've been gathering that money for decades. It's to be used in emergencies only. If we use it now, we won't have it when we need it." Timit almost sounds like the voice of reason.

Kada pipes in. "I agree. That money was to be used for special purposes, not at the whim of those who want a short-term solution."

I tap my fingers on my lap. There must be something we can do. "What about the mines around Valcora that bring in so much wealth? Why could we not buy a mine as the government? We could use the income to subsidize the people's needs. What's more, we'd be providing more jobs to those who need them."

"There are no mines for sale," Timit says.

It's like he's trying to muddle everything I do.

"I don't know," Sidle says. "Perhaps we could find one. The country is rich with them. It would provide ample opportunity to make more money."

"It's worth a try," Monkia says.

At least some are on my side.

Nash has been oddly silent. What is he thinking? I risk a glance his way, like I'm looking around the room, but it doesn't tell me anything. He's quiet and stone-like.

"Would someone like to add anything else?" I ask.

"I still say a flat tax would be best," Timit says.

"Noted." Time and time again. "Anyone else?" When the room stays silent, I know it's time to make a decision, but I'll have to ask for Timit's help since he's in charge of the money. Oh well, there's nothing to lose. If he doesn't do a good job, I can always replace him. I just don't know who with. "Having taken into consideration what you have shared with me, I would like to go ahead and leave things as they are for now. We should look into buying a mine. Timit, please see what you can do in that area. I'd be most pleased if you could find us a good deal."

He grimaces, like he tasted something bad, but he says, "I will."

"Very well, then. If there are no other concerns, I will see you all at the next council meeting." Which I can hopefully walk to.

As the council heads out of the room, I tell Nash to wait. I shouldn't meet with him alone much if it's going to cause problems, but to do that, I'll have to explain myself first. I can't have him thinking I hate him. Far from it.

When the room is clear and the door closed, he turns to me. "You wanted to speak with me?"

"You make it sound so formal." When he says nothing, I add, "Yes, well... I suppose it is."

"Ryn." The single word out of his mouth is twisted with longing and pain.

I want to reach out to him, but I stop myself. "How are you?"

Wrong question. He drops his gaze, his expression closing up. "I'm fine."

Right. "You remember that I love you?"

"I do." His gaze flickers back up to mine. "I love you as well, only I sense a *but* coming."

Unfortunately. "It's because I love you that I think we should ease off how much we appear to care for one another. It's been brought to my attention that my preference for you is widely known. I don't want to risk your life over something like that."

He brushes his thumb across my fingers, sending waves of heat through me. "Loving you is not a risk."

"Loving me is nothing but risks."

"I'll hold by your wishes to remain at bay, but that won't suppress my feelings for you." He leans closer, his breath warm on my skin. He brushes his lips against mine, the contact agonizingly short. "I will see you when you have a government job for me."

He stands and takes several steps, before I gain hold of myself. "I do have something government-related to discuss with you."

He turns and gives me an unhappy smile. "I'd best do it from over here." He takes a seat across the room from me. "What can I help you with?"

"What did you think of my idea to open a government-controlled mine?"

"As long as the workers are treated well, compensated fairly, and not too much money needs to be sunk into it, it's a fair idea."

Fair. Not what I was going for. "Do you have a better one?"

"Truth? You know what's best for this country more than you think you do. In the past months, you've spent time getting to know the people of Indell, you've changed laws for the better, and you do things to show you care about them. The only other thing you could do is maybe visit the rest of Valcora. See what your country is like outside the capital."

"It's a sound idea." Though I'm not sure I'm doing as much as he thinks I am. "Perhaps I will make a country tour in the near future. For now, would you like to join me in investigating the treasury? I've never been, and I think it's time I see what exactly my forbearers have stowed away."

"I would accompany you, but may I suggest we take someone with us if you are trying to keep up appearances? Not that I would mind spending time alone in a locked room with you."

My face heats. I clear my throat. "I'll call for Jem."

"Agreed. She'll probably know what things are worth better than either of us."

It's funny that I didn't like her when I first met her. Now her opinion is valuable, and I wish I spent more time with her. "Oh, I forgot. My leg. I can't wander anywhere just yet."

"I forgot as well. Does it hurt?"

"It's nothing." Compared to other injuries I've suffered, anyhow. "Maybe next week we can visit the treasury?"

"I'll look forward to it, and I'll let Jem know for you."

"That would be appreciated."

He heads for the door.

"Nash?"

"Yes?" He faces me.

I wish he would. I want to see his expression. "You can talk to me. About what happened."

"We've talked enough." His tone is sharp enough to pierce my heart.

Why did I think bringing up his torture would be a good idea? I should have left well enough alone. We were doing well. Now he's leaving, and it's not on good terms.

His hand is on the door knob, but he doesn't turn it. He just stands there. Finally, he says, "I'm sorry. I'll keep that in mind."

"Thank you." The knife slides out of my heart, but the wound is still there, bleeding.

CHAPTER 13

"AGAIN." The word flies from my mouth.

Jem looks up at me, sweat dripping across her face. Wilric watches her, not a bead of sweat visible.

"I don't think I'm getting it," she says.

It would be so much easier if I could show her the moves, but I'm supposed to be cautious with my leg, and I don't want to do anything that might mess up my recovery. It's hard, being down, but it'd be worse if it lasted longer. Or worse, if I was permanently disabled. "You have to keep trying. It will come," I say.

"I'm not a natural, like you."

Am I a natural, or did I train for so long that it feels that way?

"Come on, Jem." Wilric holds up his wooden sword, ready to block an attack that doesn't happen. "You've got this. You just need to keep practicing."

She growls and lunges forward. He stops her advance, knocks her sword aside, and gently taps her on the waist. With a groan, she drops the wooden sword to the ground, and her skirts swish. She wanted to change into pants, but I insisted she train in her skirt. What's the point of training her in pants when she only ever wears skirts and dresses? She needs to be able to move in them.

"We could go back to drills," Wilric says.

We've done lots of drills in the past week. I'm not sure she's up for more. Practicing the basics is important, but it gets tedious after a while. Though it's good to be able to move on instinct, I think we've done enough for now.

As if to prove my point, she grunts. Very unlady-like of her. I want to laugh, but I keep it to myself.

"You can't attack in anger. You have to be focused on the task at hand."

She doesn't appear to hear my words, instead wiping her forehead with the back of her hand. "Maybe it was a mistake to try this," she says.

"The Jem I know wouldn't give up so easily."

She sighs. "This is a lot more difficult than either of you make it look."

"That's because we've practiced so much," Wilric says. "You'll get there."

"It doesn't seem close to happening."

"You haven't been practicing a week." I keep my tone even, though I want to rage at her. That would be Daros speaking, not me, and I won't let him control me like that. He's not even here; he can't affect my actions.

"But what if we get attacked tomorrow?" she asks. "I'd be as useless as before."

Wilric picks her sword up. "I wouldn't say that."

"You have learned some basics that would help in a fight." Not against a trained assassin, but telling her that won't do any good.

Wilric sets the swords in their places in the training room, walks over to Jem, and puts a hand on her shoulder. She looks up at him with something so pure in her gaze, I have to glance away.

His words are soft but carry over to me. "You can do this. You've got the heart for it. We just need to get your skills up to where your desire is."

She sighs, more breathily than before. "I'll keep trying."

"That's the way."

I want to encourage her too, but it feels like they're having their own little moment. If I could walk stealthily, as usual, I would be out of here. Instead, I feign interest in one of my daggers, take it out, and flip it in the air before catching it again.

A minute or so later, Jem says to me, "Neat trick. Do you think I could do that?"

I stop, with the blade pointing out. "Eventually. For now, you should try again. More slowly this time, Wilric."

He nods and retrieves the practice swords. He hands one to her before getting into his fighting stance. She tries to mimic his moves and does a decent job. Her knees are bent, her head held high, and her muscles poised to strike or block. There's a tension in the lines of her body, though. A stiffness that belies her efforts.

"Begin," I say.

She attacks, and Wilric knocks her sword away. This time she recovers and brings it back up toward him, and he blocks it. I watch them go back and forth until Nash enters the room. I'm hyper-aware of him as I keep watch on the practice.

He sits on the bench close by me, but not touching me. "She's coming along."

I nod.

"You're a good teacher."

I drag my gaze away from the fight and let myself look at him. Take him in. I'm surprised he isn't off, fighting. I don't dare say that, though. "Wilric is doing most of the hard work."

"Don't sell yourself short," he says.

I press my lips together.

He tears his gaze from mine to watch them practice. "I visited my family today."

I want to gush at him. To tell him how happy I am that he finally went. Instead, I hold back and simply ask, "How are they?"

"Good. Mother has nothing but nice things to say about you. She has a bit of hero worship going on, as do my sisters."

I chuckle. "Whatever for? I've only treated them the way I've treated anyone."

"Yes, but you also saved their only son and brother's life."

The words shock me. It's the first time he's brought up the attack on his own. This is dangerous ground, and I could easily scare him away if I'm not careful. I lower my voice, so it doesn't carry, though my guards are at the far edges of the room, and Jem and Wilric are distracted by their fight. "I did it for selfish reasons."

His gaze settles intensely on me. Fiery hot. I work to keep my breathing steady, though it wants to go ragged.

"Nevertheless, they think the world of you," he says.

"And you? What do you think?"

His gaze darts to the others in the room before coming back to me. "That I can't properly thank you right now."

I can't help the grin that comes to my face. So much for keeping my distance. If anyone is watching, my feelings must be written on my face. I work to rein in my expression. "Is there something you needed?"

His eyes narrow. "Sorry. I was sent to see if you wanted the meeting in your sitting room again, or if you were well enough to make it to the council room."

He was sent. That's better than coming himself—which is ridiculous. I hate this. It's horrid to be kept from the one they love. They could have sent a servant, but didn't. It gives us an excuse to meet.

I understand why they don't want to mess with the line of succession and chance our country being destroyed by natural disasters, but it doesn't make me any happier. I glance at Wilric and Jem. It also makes no sense that my ladies-in-waiting are held to the same no-relations-or-marriage policy that I am. At least they can touch the ones they love without everyone going crazy.

"Ryn?" Nash pulls me out of my thoughts.

"Sorry. It doesn't matter. I can go to either place."

"Let's have it in the council room, then, so the advisors can come as well."

"That's fine." I focus my attention on Jem and Wilric, who are still working together. Jem lands a clumsy blow to Wilric's chest. He must have let her have that one. No way she got past his defenses on her own.

But she looks up with a smile. "Did you see that? I got him."

"I did." My voice carries through the training hall. I can't bring myself to say *well done* when it was given to her, but perhaps it will instill some confidence in her and help her do better.

She grins at Wilric. "I bet I can do it again."

"You wish." His voice carries a hint of laughter.

Nash leans over and whispers, "Is there something going on between them?"

"I'm not sure," I reply. "She has similar restrictions as I do."

His face becomes serious. "I know."

"Despite that, I think they may have feelings for each other. Or they're friendly." Which doesn't seem like either of them. They're both acting out of character. But that may be one of the things love does—changes you so you're more forthcoming with the person you care about.

I glance at Nash. Maybe less forthcoming.

Whatever is going on, I wish they could be happy, but with the existing laws, it's a faint possibility.

CHAPTER 14

MY LEG IS ONLY SLIGHTLY WEAKER than before it was wounded. As we walk down the hall toward the treasury, I think of exercises I can do to improve it. It's still tender, but strong enough for me to get back into things. Stretching it out with a walk feels good.

My guards surround me, Julina currently leading the way and Nash beside me. I haven't said a thing. I don't want anyone to get more suspicious than they already are about our relationship. Besides, my heart is sore from the blow he delivered to it.

I never thought emotional pain would be as bad as torture, but love is a different sort of torture all its own. It's not like I can exercise my heart, to make it stronger.

Our group comes to a stop outside a pair of grand doors, two guards on either side. The doors are intricately carved, gleaming under the torches lining the hall. Although it's daytime, they are needed here. There are no windows along this long corridor, which ends at the treasury and has no other halls branching off it.

One of the guards stationed by the treasury entrance pulls a torch off the wall. "Would you like me to accompany you inside the vault, Your Majesty?"

"No, thank you. My Head Advisor and I will be fine examining it on our own," I say. "My lady-in-waiting, Jem Surah, should be here shortly. Please allow her entrance when she comes. No others are allowed."

He gives a brisk nod. "You will be needing this." He hands me the torch, and another guard hands one to Nash. They station themselves back at the sides of the doors.

I pull out the key I got from Timit from around my neck. As Head of the Treasury, he is in charge of it, which makes me leery, but we'll see what's inside. He wanted to come with us, but I insisted Nash and I could do it on our own, and I'd decide if Jem would join us. It took a lot of persuasion, and in the end, I had to use my position as queen. Someday, I'd like to go over its contents with Timit, but right now I want to see its value for myself, untainted by his thoughts.

The key is thick and heavy, with lots of notches at its end. I use it to open the door, only to find a second set of doors. Nash and I move into the room and close the outer doors behind us but don't lock them. I unlock the second set with a different key and push it open.

A gasp escapes me.

Gold and gems are heaped all over the room in huge amounts. The smallest stack is more wealth than I've ever seen in one place before, and there are dozens of piles. I take several steps in. The doors close behind me. Nash must have followed me in.

I walk through the mounds that are taller than I am, making little walkways through the room. As I stare in awe, I realize there's a pattern. Around the edges are the biggest stashes. Medium-sized stashes encircle a sort of hallway. Pedestals containing smaller treasures are clustered together by in groups or scattered throughout in twos and threes.

The biggest group of pedestals hunker in the corner, surrounded by gold and gems with barely enough room to walk between them. They are about waist high and have different types of crowns and tiaras on them, ranging from overly thick with a multitude of jewels to a simple band of silver with three diamonds in the center.

As I continue to roam, I find more and more treasure, my awe growing by the moment. Most of the riches are in gold coins or gems, but here and there are piles of silver. The metal and precious stones sparkle under my torchlight.

I focus on the pedestals as I stroll through the room.

There are all sorts of interesting items. A stack of scrolls bundled together. A lamp of clear, colored glass, tall and beautiful. A strange thin needle with a bottle of what looks like ink and a bowl next to it.

I'm particularly drawn to one item, though I can't understand why. It's a simple wooden ring. Without thinking about it, I place it on the thumb of my right hand. It fits perfectly. My thumb feels warm.

"Interesting choice," Nash says, startling me.

"It's not often someone can sneak up on me."

"Today's a good day for it." He gives me a faint smile.

I peruse the dull wood on my finger. What draws me to it so? I'm reluctant to take off the ring, even if I don't understand why. Nothing about it appeals to me, visually.

"You can keep wearing it if you want," he says.

"I'm not sure I should."

"It belongs to you."

I shake my head. "It belongs to the people."

Still, it stays on my hand.

"I don't think anyone will care if you wear a plain ring taken out of the treasury."

He's right. I want to keep it, and it's nothing big. It won't hurt. "Very well."

Together, we walk. He slips his hand in mine, and I pretend everything is all right between us.

And then I see a necklace with a green jewel.

I gasp.

"What is it?" Concern laces his words.

It's the First Queen's necklace. I'm uncertain about touching it, a feeling holding me back the same way something wanted me to take the ring. Perhaps it's reverence for the First Queen and all that she's done for me. Guiding me through this job as queen, listening to me, and being there for me when I needed someone.

Nash looks from me to the necklace. "Ryn?"

"Sorry. I'm just surprised." Do I tell him about the First Queen? I shouldn't; I don't want him to think I'm crazy. Then again, this is Nash. I don't want to lie to him or hide things from him. Maybe I should have told him sooner. "This necklace belonged to the First Queen of Valcora."

He furrows his eyebrows. "How do you know? I didn't think anyone knew much about her."

I lick my lips. "I've seen her. She comes to me, in something similar to a dream, ever since I first drank the Mortum Tura."

His expression remains so neutral, I can't tell what he's thinking.

"Do you think I'm crazy?" I ask.

He glances around the room as if to make certain we're alone. "No. I think you've been touched by powerful magic."

He believes me.

A rush of relief floods through me. He believes me. "That's what she said. Well... not powerful, but she said it was the magic of the Mortum Tura that allowed me to speak with her."

He runs a hand through his hair. "Ryn, I haven't heard of anything like this. If the country found out..."

"What?"

"I don't know how they'd react. It's either brilliant or dangerous."

A chill permeates the air. "How could it be dangerous?"

He takes a step closer, lowering his voice. "Magic is uncommon in Valcora."

"I know, but why does that make it dangerous?"

"Maybe it doesn't. Maybe I'm wrong. But sometimes people react poorly to things they don't understand."

It is true that I had a hard time with my first experience with the First Queen. It's easy to see how others would have a difficult time with it, especially since they can't interact with her. "That's part of the reason I never told anyone about her. I'm not always sure I haven't gone crazy."

"You're perfectly sane. No one understands much about the Mortum Tura. I'm not surprised it does more than we first suspected," he says. "What is she like?"

"She's wise, most of the time. Sometimes helpful, but often leaves me to figure out things on my own. She says she's here to guide me. To keep me from wanting..."

"Wanting what?"

I don't wish to tell him, but his expression is so earnest. "To kill myself."

His eyes widen slightly, but otherwise he doesn't react.

It feels strange to tell someone, even if that someone is him, but I need to show him I can open up. "You know some of what I went through with Daros."

Daros. What would he think of this treasure? He'd love to get his hands on it. I force myself to stay focused on the conversation. "It was hard, for lack of a better word. After I left, I kept thinking about all I did for him. The people I killed. The blood on my hands. I couldn't take it anymore. I wanted to end my life."

"Oh Ryn..." He gives my hand a gentle squeeze.

If I stop, I'll never get it all out, so I continue. "I never mattered to anyone other than for what I was worth as an assassin. For once, I needed to matter. To be the focus. What better way than the Mortum Tura? Only I didn't count on the fact that the drink only chooses a queen who doesn't want to be queen."

He raises his eyebrows. "What?"

I nod. "It's true. The queen is someone who doesn't wish to be queen. Who doesn't want power. Which is one reason why the

First Queen left her essence in the potion. She knew most of us girls who became queen would be desperate and need guidance and help."

"What an awful plan."

I bristle. "Why awful? I thought it was smart to have only someone who didn't want to be queen make it. Less power-hungry rulers that way."

"That's true, but what a horrible experience for all those girls who simply wanted to be queen, and instead died a horrific death."

The First Queen's presences feels close, as if I've drawn her attention. I find myself wanting to defend her. "It was the only way the potion would work."

"Maybe. But it doesn't lessen the lives lost."

"No. It doesn't." It's uncomfortably hot in here, the chill gone. The summer sun must be shining down on this part of the building. I have to change the subject. I can't abide talking about death any longer. "This is why I don't have nightmares anymore. The First Queen stops them."

"Wish she could stop them for me too," he mutters.

"I wish the same." It's my turn to give his hand a squeeze. "Will you do me a favor and keep her a secret?"

"I will." There's a note of hesitancy in his voice, but I don't push it.

"Have you ever seen anything like this?" I whisper, waving at the room around us.

"Never."

"We could use this for the country. There's plenty here. We can feed the people and build things that they need." I raise my voice with excitement, but I don't care. "Jem should be here soon to help us know how much value these things have, but even without her, I can tell there's more than enough."

Nash scans what we can see of the room again, his enthusiasm reined in. "We could feed the people, but you have to remember you're ruler over an entire nation. This may look like a lot of money—and make no mistake, it is—but with a whole country to take care of, the gold would go fast."

My shoulders drop. "You're right. Of course you are. I only hoped…"

"I know."

Another thought perks me up. "If we can't give it to them outright, we should be able to invest it back into them."

"That is an excellent plan, only how will you go about it?"

"We can use it to buy a mine, like I talked about before, or on other projects to need done. Create jobs and make a better life for everyone. I'm sure we can think of something."

I stare at the piles of treasure surrounding me. We'd better be able to think of something.

CHAPTER 15

I GLANCE OUT THE WINDOW, waiting for Timit. I'd be much more comfortable if Nash was here, but I didn't think Timit would take me as seriously if I had someone figuratively holding my hand. Besides, I know how to live without comfort, even if I prefer it.

Soon a servant comes to the door and announces Timit. He glides into the room—as much as a large man can glide—bows, and takes the seat at my right. I'm grateful there's space between the chairs as I don't want to be overly close to him.

As soon as the door closes, he says, "You wished to see me, Your Majesty?"

"Yes. I've seen something that concerns you." I leave it at that to see if he's going to say anything. Long ago, I learned not to let silence bother me, but it can make others uncomfortable.

At first, the quiet doesn't seem to get to him. I'm about to talk, when he fidgets in his chair. The lack of sound is taking its toll. Just a minute more.

"What is it that concerns me, Your Majesty?" His fidgeting lessens but doesn't completely subside.

I don't reply right away. His eye twitches. Good. Hopefully, he's more pliable than usual.

"You've been keeping things from me," I say.

"I can't imagine what you're speaking of."

Again, I hesitate. "Don't worry so much. If it was serious, I'd have you replaced." Somewhat of an idle threat. I don't know who to replace him with that has experience, or I'd have done so already. Still, he swipes at his forehead like he's sweating. "Is there something you think I ought to have been told?"

He swipes at his forehead like he's sweating. "I can't imagine what Your Majesty means."

"Nothing at all?"

"There... erm... are enough taxes coming in to handle the workings of the government. Most of what you're planning on anyway. I believe the taxes are too high on the Kurah. They are what drives our economy. We need to feed them, not starve them."

I remain expressionless. "I know. I read through the reports you prepared."

"Oh." He twists a ring on one of his stubby fingers. "Is this a problem, then?"

"It's not what I want to discuss with you," I say.

"What else is there?"

Either he's good at hiding it, or he doesn't think the treasury was of much significance. "What I want to know is why there is so much in the treasury and why you've been hiding it?"

His eyebrows raise, but he doesn't look scared. "I didn't know you were unaware of the amount of money the treasury holds. I thought it was common knowledge."

"Who else knows about it, then?"

"Well... I can't be certain."

"What do you mean?"

"I thought people knew. I've known for so long, nothing else has crossed my mind."

"So you haven't told anyone?"

"No."

Interesting. "How long have you been doing this job?"

"About twenty-five years."

I knew he was older than me, but not that old. No wonder he's so set in his position. How many queens has he seen come and go, while he's stayed in his position?

"If we're going to continue working together, I need you to have a more open mind," I say.

His thick lips pinch together. He's not at all happy with the idea. "You'd do well to take my advice, from the experience I've gained over those years, Your Majesty."

Maybe. Maybe not. "I understand this will be hard for you, but it needs to be done. Otherwise, I will replace you."

He sputters and finally says, "I will work on that, Your Majesty."

"Good." We'll see if he does. "Now, do you have any news about a mine we could purchase?"

"I would strongly encourage you to consider lowering the taxes for the Kurah, Your Majesty."

"If we can bring enough revenue in from or mines another source, I will consider such a thing."

His eyebrows jump. "Thank you."

Never thought I'd hear those two words from him. Maybe he isn't so bad, but stuck in his ways. "The mine?"

He clears his throat. "I will get more serious about looking for one, Your Majesty."

I resist the urge to roll my eyes. "Be sure that you do. That is all for today."

He stands and gives a better bow than I've seen him give, though it's still stiff. As he exits, a servant enters and says, "Shillian Nilmac is here to see you, Your Highness."

Of course she is. Yet a part of me is excited to see her. "Send her in."

The servant bows and leaves, and a moment later, Shillian arrives. "Thank you for seeing me." She takes a seat next to me, even as she continues talking. "That was so frightening, when we were attacked, but you were incredible. I've never seen anything like it. How's your leg?" She's been saying the same things ever since I was attacked.

"It's almost back to normal."

"I'm so glad to hear that. I wish I could give you a hug and make things better. What would you like to do today? If you're not busy, that is."

The hug part makes me want to cry, though I don't understand why. I hurry the conversation on, unwilling to let tears build in my eyes. "I don't know if I have time for anything today. It's pretty busy."

"I understand. You are the queen. I never thought I'd be the mother of the queen. I'm so proud of the lady you've become."

I can't help it; I have to ask. "You know I'm an assassin?"

She drops her gaze to her hands. "I heard that. Yes." Her gaze returns to mine, eyes blazing. "But it doesn't matter."

I want to reach out and squeeze her hand, but I resist. "Thank you."

She nods.

"Where's Carver today?" I ask.

"He's out, looking for a job."

"Best of luck with it."

"He'll appreciate that."

"There's something I've been wanting to ask, and I have a little time before going to my meetings," I say. "How did you and Carver meet?" Because I don't know much about them, though we've spent some time together.

Her cheeks turn a light shade of pink. "We grew up together. Lived in the same neighborhood most of our childhood. When his parents died, he took off on his own but always came back to visit me. I don't remember when we started to fall in love. One day, I realized I did love him and had for some time. Shortly after that, he proposed, and we were married."

"What was the wedding like?" I've never been to one. I haven't a clue how they happen.

"Simple. An officer of the state, given power by the queen, married us in a simple ceremony. My parents and a few friends were there, but there was so much work to be done, even then, that we didn't do much to celebrate. I still had washing to do, and Carver had just gotten a job as a mason."

My dream of a romantic union is dashed. Though I suppose it is nice that they have known each other since childhood. Friends turned to lovers. I wanted a spark of something more to make me believe there was hope for me.

But there isn't.

Nash and I can never be.

CHAPTER 16

THE FIRST QUEEN FROWNS. *Have I seen her frown before? Perhaps, but not like this. I have the distinct feeling I did something to upset her.*

She sighs. "It's true. I am a little upset."

"Why?" *I tramp down my other thoughts. I don't want to unwittingly disturb her more.*

"If you must know, I'm slightly perturbed you told Nash about me." She crosses her ankles, her green dress swishing.

"I didn't think you'd mind. He's good at keeping secrets."

"I hope you're right. I'd hate to have a witch hunt after you."

Would that really happen?

She primly sets her hands together in her lap. "Difficult to say. Magic is mysterious in Valcora during these times. Only the Mortum Tura remains, and it's been here for so long, people are accustomed to it."

"Mysterious, yes, but a witch hunt?" *It doesn't feel true, but then again, Nash did say it might be dangerous.*

"I'm not certain either, but there's a chance it might come to that. I don't want to take that chance on you when you're finally starting to make a difference for the country."

"You think it's a good idea to use the money to create jobs? To buy a

mine, so we can delve into the natural resources Valcora has to offer?"
I ask.

"Trust your instincts."

I relax. If she and Nash both think it's a good idea, I may be on to something. What are my instincts? I search deep inside, for what I'm feeling. I almost get the impression I shouldn't be investing the money back into the nation. That it would hurt, more than help. But that can't be right, can it? I shove the feelings away. "I will do this."

"I can tell you want to achieve great things."

Heat rises to my cheeks. I look off into the distance, the colors of the sunset blurring together.

"You should be proud of what you're accomplishing, not hiding from it."

"Maybe." I've never been pleased in a job well done. There's always something not perfect about it. Something to improve on. Daros constantly reminded me of that.

"He is not what you should be judging yourself by. He is a despicable man, who thrives on destroying others."

It's hard to believe that I shouldn't judge myself. I hurry to talk before she can comment on that thought as well. "He's still out there. I wish we could find him."

"He's sneaky. Hopefully, he's run off to another country by now."

"It's possible, but unlikely. He likes to get his way, and he hasn't. Something bad will come of it."

"You're strong. If he comes back, you'll handle him."

I should take the opportunity to think about that. What will I do with him when he comes back? He needs to die, but I promised myself to kill no more. I broke that promise once. I don't want to do it again.

"But if it's what's best, maybe you should."

"We'll see when the time comes." I'm slightly annoyed at her reading my thoughts, but tamp it down so she won't be offended. Though I wonder..."Can I read your thoughts as you read mine?"

The skin around her eyes tightens. "No one's ever tried."

I find that surprising. It seems like a natural thing to do.

"Only because you think differently than other queens."

The statement gives me pause. "In a good way or bad? No. You know what? Don't answer that. Let me try to read your mind. If it doesn't bother you, that is?"

"Go ahead."

I concentrate on her, trying to discover her thoughts. Searching for a hint of her mind out there in the dark abyss. I hunt for it, pushing myself to find a scrap of anything. It doesn't do any good. The way isn't as clear at all. "I'm getting nothing."

She gives a slight nod.

"I may not be able to read your thoughts, but are you worried about something?" *I ask.*

"You caught that?" *Her tone is as smooth as usual, giving nothing away.*

"I did." *What could she possibly be worried about, in a dreamlike state such as this?*

She sighs. "I didn't want to bother you with it, but it's left over from speaking about Daros. I'm not sure what to do about him. He's become quite a pain, and if you think he hasn't left the country—that he's going to stick around and do more damage—I believe you."

Is that what's bothering her? Her expression is once again hard to read, so I go with what she said. She has no reason to lie, and it makes perfect sense. "That makes two of us," *I tell her.*

"We can both think about it and see if we come up with anything."

"I'll try," *I say.* "I've been meaning to ask you about your necklace. I saw it in the treasury."

"You found it. I was wondering if you ever would."

"You knew it was there?"

"I suspected. Other queens went in the treasury and saw it. I guessed it wasn't removed."

"But you didn't know?"

"Not for certain. Why such interest in my necklace?"

I'm not sure exactly. "I think it has something to do with proving that you exist."

"You doubt still?"

"No. It's good to have a reminder, though." I pause before plunging forward. "Does your necklace do anything special?"

"What do you mean?"

I shrug. "There was something about it when I saw it."

"Perhaps it was reverence and respect for it, knowing it belonged to me."

"Maybe." But I have a feeling she's being evasive. Why? I try to clamp down on that thought, but it's too late.

"Why would I be evasive with you? I have no to reason to be." She doesn't sound hurt, but neither does she look happy.

I shrug. "It's an old habit, from being with Daros. I'm not used to people being up front with me yet."

"You can trust me. You know that, don't you?"

I search my feelings. Warmth and sweetness encompass me. "I do."

"Good. I want us to be on the same team. That can't occur if we don't trust each other."

"What happens when a queen isn't on your side?" Though I don't plan on going that way myself, I am curious what would happen with someone like that, having the First Queen stuck in their head with no way to escape.

"Like Deedra?"

The queen before me. "Yes. What was that like for the both of you?"

"When a person doesn't fit with my plans, it's... trying."

"I can't imagine being stranded in someone's thoughts and not getting along with them."

She gives a thin smile. "It's not easy. Some people are more enjoyable than others by nature. It's not something I like to think about."

"I'm sorry. I don't mean to bring up difficult topics for you."

"It's fine. I know you have a curious mind."

Too curious for my own good. Daros smashed a lot of it out of me, but it seems to be coming back more than I'd expect.

"It's about time for you to wake up for the day. Anything else you'd like to ask before you go?"

"Will you always be here, helping me?"

She smiles—a wide, bright expression. "I will."

"Thank you for your guidance."

"Always."

CHAPTER 17

INKGA IS PINNING my hair up for the day. We ate breakfast together, discussing her new clothing designs, which I'm excited to see. It's funny how comfortable I've become with her around. The only other person I'm like this with is Nash, and that's entirely different.

Either way, I don't feel the need to constantly watch her. If she ever schemes to kill me, it'll be far too easy. Though I doubt it. There was a spider in my bedroom the other day, and she couldn't bring herself to smash it.

"There," she says. "All ready for the day. What plans do you have?"

"I don't have much scheduled today. I'll probably find lots to keep me busy." I turn to face her. "I have to be honest—this place is wonderful, but I'm getting tired of it."

"You could always go on a tour of the country." She sets my brush on the vanity.

"Could I really?" Nash mentioned something like that, but I didn't think much about it, like I should have.

"Queens sometimes do such a thing. The nation would enjoy

seeing you, and you seem like the type of queen who'd enjoy visiting other cities and meeting your countrymen."

"That sounds much better than meeting after meeting."

"I'm sure there will still be meetings, only more spread out."

And they won't include the likes of Timit. Plus, if I go around the country, Daros won't be there unless he follows me around. He always preferred to stay in the city. "Who do I need to speak with to make this happen?"

She grins. "I'd be happy to get things moving for you. When do you want to go?"

"As soon as arrangements can be made. Let's get Jem to help. She was probably trained on just such a thing."

"I'll get her and alert Nash to your intentions."

She hurries out. I check to make certain I have all my daggers and that my poison pouch is around my neck, and then I make my way to my usual seat in the sitting room.

I want to take Nash with me. I hope he wants to go. Maybe I should leave him in charge, but he's not himself. I'll take Inkga, and I should take Shillian and Carver. Anyone else who wants to go and can be ready in time will be welcome.

I continue to go over a list of security plans and people who should come in my head until Jem and Inkga return a few minutes later. I tell them my thoughts.

Jem laughs. "You are eager to see the countryside." When I give her a flat expression, she adds, "Your Majesty."

"I thought we were past that." I sigh. Too many of my thoughts have apparently been written on my face. "Truth is, I am eager."

"Good. We can work with that. We should be able to go in a day or two, but we'll have to travel slowly at first."

"Why?"

"So there's time for the towns to be alerted to your arrival. The first thing we'll do is make a schedule of where you're going when, and Kada will let them know we're coming. Arrangements will be made. There will be some form of a party or celebration in at least a few of the towns."

"That's unnecessary."

Her mouth tightens. "You may think so, but the people do not."

"Very well." I don't want to cause them more trouble, but I did enjoy dancing with them before spotting Daros in the crowd. Was he there, or did my fears make him up? "Very well."

"Good. The country will be eager to see their queen, though considering certain recent events and the fact that Daros in still on the loose, Jaku will presumably not wish you to go. I'm sure we can convince him, if you take enough guards."

"As many as he sees fit. I don't want the palace unguarded, though."

She nods. "He'll know."

I suppose I need to leave someone in charge while I'm gone. "I'd like you to see to things while I'm away."

"Me?" She puts a hand to her chest, eyebrows slightly raised.

"You know the country well, and the laws even better. What's more, you know more about protocol than I ever will. Will you accept this assignment?"

She gives a small curtsy. "I'd be delighted, Your Majesty."

All this *Your Highness, my lady,* and *Your Majesty* will most likely increase again as I go around those who don't know how much it bothers me. Oh well. It's becoming more of a background noise.

"And you will come with me, Inkga, if you so desire."

"It would be an honor." She also curtsies but doesn't add an honorific, much to my delight. "We'll have to look at your wardrobe, to see what will be fitting for travel and what will be good to meet the people in."

"Pants for traveling, please. You can pick whatever you think is best as long as I can still have my daggers."

Inkga smiles. "Sounds good."

"I'll make arrangements," Jem says.

"Send Jaku to me," I reply. "I want to tell him myself."

She nods and leaves the room.

"Thank you for agreeing to go with me," I tell Inkga.

"Truthfully, it is an honor. I'm so excited, Ryn. Most of my life has been spent in this palace, and I have never been outside of Indell. I'd love to see more than just this place. Meet new people. Make new friends."

"You will." And with any luck, so will I.

We discuss different cities for a while, when a servant knocks at the door and introduces Jaku. My Head of Guard strides in the room, gives a bow, and waits with one hand resting on the hilt of his sword.

"Thank you for coming. I am going to be traveling the country. I would like you to arrange as many men you feel are necessary to make that happen, while still keeping the palace guarded."

His expression remains hard. "Forgive me, Your Majesty, but I believe the safest course of action would be to remain here at the palace."

I give him a level stare. "Let's be honest."

"Of course."

"How many attacks have happened while I'm here at the palace?"

"The exact number is hard to guess," he says.

"Because it's high?"

"Yes," he grumbles.

"And you think it will be higher outside these walls?"

"It already has been. Almost every time you go out, you are attacked."

True. Not a comforting fact. "But we won't be staying in the city. Don't you think it'd be different in other towns?"

His lips form a thin line.

"Don't you?" I prod.

"It's difficult to say. They could have better access to you than they do inside these walls."

"But…"

He sighs. "But other towns may not be as hostile to you, according to my sources."

"You keep track of how other towns feel about me?"

"I do. My job is to protect you from all threats. I need to know about the entire country to do that."

Interesting. "It would be safe for me to go, then."

"I said *not as hostile*. They haven't had direct reports of you like the people in Indell have. They don't know about issues until after they're fixed, and they usually get news of the fix with it. There's still some animosity toward you. The Kurah may be a problem, and Daros may follow you, thinking he can get you in a less guarded place."

Oh, joy. "I've had to fight for my life in this very palace. I think it's safe to assume things will be dangerous wherever I go. With your guards at my side, I'm certain I'll be fine."

"I'm not certain, which is why I'm hesitant," he says. "But I can see you're set on going, so I'll have to make sure you have enough protection."

"Thank you." I keep myself from grinning like a fool.

I'll send word to Carver and Shillian to see if they're interested in joining me. Now the only one I need to talk to is Nash. What if he refuses to come? He needs to join us because that's where all the guards will be. I want him safe from Daros's clutches.

* * *

"I'D BE happy to join you," Nash says.

That was easier than I expected. "Good."

"When do we leave?'

"As soon as arrangements can be made."

He relaxes back into his seat. "Who will be coming with us?"

"Inkga, guards, Shillian, Carver, and anyone else who wishes to come."

He sighs.

"What's wrong?"

"Nothing."

"Something is. Tell me."

He gives me a weak smile. "I'd like to spend some time alone with you. There are always others about."

Which means I can't pay much attention to him. The thought warms my cheeks and has me wanting to move closer. "You have me alone now."

His gaze sends a blaze of fire through me. "And I intend to make full use of it, like I should have been doing all along."

He leans in closer. My heart flutters. We're going to kiss.

I haven't felt his lips against mine in too long a time.

His breath is warm against my lips. Sweet. He is focused on me, no hint of fear clouding his eyes. I have waited for this to happen since he came back to me. There may be greater hope than I thought.

I can almost feel his kiss when there's a knock on the door.

We bolt apart, heaving for air.

Nash takes a moment to look me over before answering the door. A servant says, "Shillian and Carver Nilmac, Your Majesty."

The announced two come in, gushing about the trip. I want to shove them both outside, slam the door, and get back to our kiss. Why did they have to come now?

Shillian says, "I'm so grateful you invited us to tour the countryside with you. I've spent most of my life in Indell. It will be wonderful to see other areas for a change."

She continues spouting off, but I have a hard time focusing. I'm only aware of him—Nash. The warmth that so abruptly left. The almost-kiss between us. That's what I want—his lips against mine.

And if anyone knew, Nash would be dead.

CHAPTER 18

THE MORNING DAWNS bright and early, but I spend most of it waiting.

Finally, a servant says, "Your carriage is ready, my lady."

I thought it would never get here. "Thank you."

I head out the front door, grateful for the pants Inkga designed for stashing daggers and poisons on my person. Whenever I've gone out of the city for a job, I like to feel prepared.

My carriage is surrounded by a good thirty guards on horseback. Someone is over-prepared. Jaku waits at the carriage door.

When I get to him, I say, "Going overboard, don't you think?"

"Not when it comes to your safety."

"Better be careful, or someone may think you believe I'm doing a good job." I climb in the carriage before he can respond.

He mutters something under his breath.

"What was that?"

He closes the carriage door, talking through the window. "Nothing, Your Highness."

I chuckle as he goes to a nearby unoccupied horse. I turn my attention to my carriage mates. I have a seat to myself, and we're spaced farther apart than in a usual carriage, so no one is in danger of

JANEAL FALOR

touching me. Across from me are Inkga and Inyi. My lady-in-waiting decided she wanted to join us, though she's the only one. At least she said she wanted to go with us. More likely, it was believed *proper*.

"Ready for the long ride, Your Majesty?" Inyi asks.

"As much as one can be ready for such a thing." I'd rather walk or ride.

Nash was lucky to get a horse despite being my Head Advisor. In another carriage, Shillian and Carver are coming along with Kada. As Head of Relations for the Queen, she deemed it necessary to join us.

Another council member joining us is Sidle, my Head of Military. He's riding a horse with the guard. I don't know what prompted this, and I probably won't have much interaction with him. I'm glad to have some members of the council with me, though.

Several extra carriages were provided for all the luggage. I didn't dare look at how much Inkga packed for me. Probably too much, and combined with everyone else's things, it was a lot.

The ride is filled with chatter between Inyi and Inkga. I remain quiet, eager to get to our destination. Though it will be at a passing inn, I'm anxious to meet the people there. I'm even more anxious to meet people in the rest of the country. My stomach churns a little, and I wonder if it's because of the apprehension of meeting the people or the carriage ride. Maybe both.

The countryside is beautiful, my mountains always in the distance. Their steep slopes and close proximity make for a breathtaking view. The fields leading up to them are golden and bright, their harvest ready to be picked.

When we get to the inn, the carriage door opens, and I'm the first to step out. Jaku is scanning the area, and I'm surrounded by guards and one other woman. She's not plump enough to be considered fashionable in the capital, but she's still more well-rounded than me. Her lips are painted a deep red, and her golden brown eyes seem friendly. That alone makes me not want to trust them.

At least I recognize I have trust issues?

"Welcome to my humble inn." The woman curtsies. "I am Greeta. I've prepared rooms for you and your companions—the best we have to offer. I hope you enjoy them. Would you like dinner sent up or in the main room?"

"Sent up, if you would, Greeta. Thank you."

She blushes a pretty pink that makes her look younger. "It is my pleasure. I will get your food ready. Please follow my serving girl to your rooms." She motions to a crooked-toothed, brown-eyed girl, who gives a shy smile after a curtsy.

We follow the serving girl inside the inn and up the stairs as Greeta goes deeper into the main floor. The girl stops at a room three flights up and opens the door. "For Her Majesty."

Jaku and Afet check the room, making sure there are no hidden issues. While we wait, I try not to tap my foot. I just want food and sleep. The day was longer day than I thought it would be. Plus I've become spoiled to the way of life at the palace. It's no wonder I've put on weight.

Jaku and Afet exit the room. Jaku says, "It's clear, Your Majesty."

I nod my thanks before entering the room and searching it for myself. Inkga and Julina follow me in while the rest of the party moves on to find their own rooms. No sight of Nash, but I know he's around. I'll have to get used to seeing less of him.

As soon as I'm certain there's no threat, I plop down onto the bed. "Ow."

"Are you all right?" Inkga asks.

I pull myself up and rub my lower back. "This bed is not fit for sleeping." And it's supposed to be the best in the inn. Hopefully, the others aren't as picky as I've become. Comforts in life are something I do enjoy, but tonight it'll be the floor.

"I can switch rooms," Inkga says. "See if there's something else that would be more to your liking."

"It's fine. I'll manage."

The food arrives, and thankfully, it's better than the bed. Once we've all eaten, I go to the window and look out on the moons. The red one is out, but the others have yet to make an appearance. I focus my gaze on the stars, their twinkling light brighter here than in the city.

"They're beautiful out here." Inkga comes up beside me.

"Agreed." I turn toward her. She has a gleam of happiness in her eyes. "You've never been out of Indell before? Not even a little ways?"

She doesn't take her eyes off the sky. "Nope. I didn't go into Indell that often either, so I know very few places around it. I know the palace well, though."

"I'm glad I brought you along."

She finally looks at me, the sparkle in her eyes brighter than ever. "I'm glad you brought me, too."

I get my night gown on behind a dressing curtain while Inkga takes a turn in the bath. When she's done, I ask Julina, "Aren't you going to change?"

"Not right now."

"Are you going to sleep in your clothes?"

"If that's what it takes to keep you safe." She's so serious; I want to laugh. Of course, I don't dare insult her.

"This was a spur-of-the-moment trip. I don't think anyone will be expecting us to bring trouble yet. Besides, if they do, I can handle myself long enough for you to get in your sleep clothes."

She puts a hand on the hilt of her sword but stays silent.

"Suit yourself." I'm not going to force her to if she doesn't want to.

Inkga pulls down the covers of the bed meant for me before going to a couch near a cold fireplace.

"You can sleep on the bed if you want. Either of you." I grab a pillow from the bed and throw it on the ground. I lie down while Inkga's eyes grow wide and Julina gives a small smile.

A moment later, Inkga says, "What are you doing?"

"Sleeping."

"On the floor?" The horror in her voice sounds like she just woke up from a nightmare.

I shrug. "Better than that bed. Though maybe you'll find it to your liking."

"A queen can't sleep on the floor."

"I've done it before."

"That was different. You've grown as a queen since then."

I fluff the pillow behind my head and give her a grin. "Good night."

She sputters before calming herself. "Well, if you're going to leave me the bed, I'll take it." She walks to it and lies down. Julina makes herself a little bed under the window. Moments later, Inkga crawls off the bed. "You win. That thing is atrocious."

"Maybe the couch is preferable?" I ask.

"You should sleep there, then."

"No, the floor is fine."

"All right." She settles onto the couch and is breathing heavily before I have a chance to ask if it's any better. It must be doing the job.

There's a shifting outside my door. The guards, probably. I know Jaku planned on stationing at least four of them. Too many, but no one asked me. I suppose Jaku knows what he's doing.

The night is warm enough that I don't need a blanket, despite not having a fire and the lateness of the season. Still, I toss and turn. The hardness of the ground is worse than I remember, but that's not what keeps me awake.

Daros.

Being on a wooden floor reminds me of him. Of the way he used to treat me.

I reach over, rip the blankets off the bed, and arrange them beneath me. When I lie back down, it's not as bad. Despite that, I continue tossing and turning. When I turn toward the window, I find Julina's gaze on me.

"Are you all right?" she whispers.

"You should be asleep." By the light of the moons coming in the window, it's gotten late.

"So should you."

"Just thinking."

"Do you want to talk about it?" she asks.

"No. Thank you." Though something does come to mind. "Why did you choose to become a guard?"

She sighs. "No one has ever asked me that."

"Never?"

She shakes her head. "I suppose it was obvious to those who came in around the same time as me. They either were from a rich family but not in a position to inherit or most of them were like me—from a family trying to recover from the famine. My parents made so little that, when I was old enough, I chose to join the guard. It was the only way to help them."

"They must appreciate that."

She stares at the ceiling. "The truth is, with ten children in my family, I'm barely missed, even if they do use my pay."

"I'm sorry."

"Don't be. It's the way things are."

Doesn't mean it's impossible to feel bad about her situation. I can't imagine what it would be like to have brothers and sisters, but I know what it's like to not be missed. To have no one who really cares.

She doesn't look at me again, though she doesn't close her eyes.

CHAPTER 19

I TALK to the First Queen about politics and what I should expect while visiting other cities in Valcora. It's nice to rest and have someone to talk these things over with who won't judge me and can't tell others my inner thoughts.

The next morning Inkga packs up, and Julina disappears. Eldim comes in her stead. We have breakfast, get back into the carriage, and head out to our destination. The ride is much like yesterday's, with me staring out the window while the other two talk.

About an hour from our destination, we stop at a little house, where I change out of my traveling clothes and into something more fitting what people expect a queen to be wearing. It's still too subdued for Inyi, but I like it. No flounces, giant skirts, or lace.

Back in the carriage, I eagerly stare at the changing scenery, the houses growing more and more frequent. Will the citizens like me? Will they have heard bad things about me and want to kill me so they can have a new queen? A better one?

I shove the thoughts from my mind.

When we arrive, my fingers are sore from being pinched and

unpinched. The door to the carriage opens, and I steel myself before pasting a smile on my face and climbing out.

The first thing I notice is Nash. I let my gaze slide over him, not wanting to show favoritism. The scenery is full of wild colors. People wearing bright blues, greens, reds, yellows, and purples are watching my every move as I climb out of the carriage.

It's surprisingly silent, gazes intent on me. I step carefully. No sense tripping in front of this huge gathering. As soon as I get both feet on the ground, they all bow low to the ground. They move like a ripple, almost as far as I can see.

"Please rise." The people are everywhere. This is supposed to be one of the biggest cities on my royal tour. I believe it. Riding in, we saw lots of buildings and crowds watching us from the side of the road. This isn't a city I've been to as the Shadow Wraith. It's a pleasant thought. The first time I'm here, it's as *Ryn. Queen Ryn*, unfortunately, but much better than as an assassin.

My guards admit a woman before closing the gap back up. She has her hair done up in an elaborate braid and wears a shocking-yellow dress, her green eyes taking in more than I'd like. She bows to me, and I motion for her to get up.

"Welcome to Pulfa, Queen Ryn," she says. "We are honored by your presence. I am Opla Kindor, ruler of this fine city."

"Thank you for hosting us." For once, I'm grateful for all the time I spent with my ladies-in-waiting.

"I assure you, it is our pleasure. Please come and get yourself situated before we host a dinner for you this evening."

Is it my imagination, or are her hands shaking? "That would be nice."

She points to the building on our left. "This is our finest inn. The innkeeper has prepared a room for you and your company."

"We're thankful for your generosity," Nash says from my left side.

When did he move closer? How did I not notice? There are too many people here. Too much going on. I'll be grateful to get to my room.

I introduce Nash to Opla. She holds out her hand for him to kiss. A surge of jealousy rips through me, but I force my expression to remain neutral. Nash is trustworthy, even if that's hard for me to comprehend.

It's that she can openly have his kisses, when I can have nothing.

I tear myself away from those thoughts. They'll do me no good. Nor will they do her any good, since I feel like punching her in the face.

My smile is tight, but at least it's there.

I slink my way forward, careful not to touch anyone. Opla and Nash traipse behind me, guards surrounding us. I hope Inkga is coming, but I don't glance back and show the weakness of wanting a certain person by me.

As we come to the inn, a man stands to one side of the door, a woman beside him. The rest of the crowd moves out of the way of my guards, but those two stay in place. They're both round, with green tunics on. They're about the same height—a little taller than me. The woman scowls at me, but the man grins ear to ear.

When we reach them, the man says, "Welcome to the Boar's Inn. It's a pleasure to serve you, my lady. Your rooms are ready and we've drawn baths in all of them. Please, feel free freshen up and then we will have a celebration of your arrival."

"Thank you." My mouth is tired of saying that. I'll probably have to keep saying it as long as I'm traveling. I'd much rather have reason to pull my daggers out. Even Daros would be a welcome relief. Not really, everything just feels different than I'm used to. Did he follow us out here once he learned of my coming, or is he waiting like a tiger to spring on Indell while I'm gone?

There's no reason to fret. Jem and Wilric will take good care of the place while I am gone. I trust them. They've earned at least that much.

The inn is what I anticipated—lots dull brown wood, tables surrounded by chairs all over the ground floor, and a staircase up the side. The only thing missing is customers, but that's because I'm here.

The innkeeper and who I assume is his wife lead the way up the stairs. We pass by several doors. When we come to one in the middle of the hallway, the innkeeper pulls out a key and unlocks it.

"This is your room, Your Majesty," the innkeeper says.

He hands the key to Inkga, who appeared out of nowhere. Julina scouts out the room before motioning us inside.

I can feel Nash's gaze on my back, but I don't turn and acknowledge him. As much as I want to, I can't.

There's a sense of relief that comes with the door closing. The only ones I have to perform for are Julina and Inkga, and the two of them are hardly a concern. I plop down on the nearest chair, wishing I didn't change into a dress before we got here. Inkga insisted it would look better if I didn't arrive in my traveling clothes, but it's so much more restrictive than a good pair of pants.

The room is much better appointed than I expected from the inn. This must be their best room, or they made it nicer because they knew I was coming, which would be kind of them.

A huge bed takes up most of one wall. Across from it, next to where I'm sitting, is a couch with a small table to the side of it, sitting in front of an unlit fire. In the corner is a dressing screen, which I assume is hiding the bath. On the other wall, there's a large window with a vanity close by.

"Do you want to bathe before the water gets cold?" Inkga asks.

"You two should go first. I don't mind cold water." It's all I had growing up. Though I've enjoyed being spoiled by warm water more recently.

"Forgive me, but I believe that would be inappropriate." Inkga moves around the room, gathering things needed for a bath, like soap and clothes, and putting them behind the dressing screen.

"Julina?" I ask.

"After you, Your Majesty. Besides, I should get someone else to stand guard while I bathe."

I wave away her concern. "I can guard myself. We're safe enough here." Guards must be posted outside the door. The window is the only concern. While it's possible for someone to come in that way, it probably won't happen. I'm sure guards are posted there as well. Either way, I'm prepared for it anyway.

But if both girls are going to refuse a bath before me, I'd better hurry to save them some warm water. "Fine. I'll go first, but know I'm not doing it willingly. And Julina, I will be considered the guard while you get rid of your travel dust."

She has the gall to roll her eyes. I like her better for it.

After a quick bath, Inkga has me change into a dress that has more leeway than the last one—but is still a dress. It's a dark blue with a slash showing white in the skirt and more slashes in the arms. The important part is the amount of daggers I can stash on my person, hidden from sight. It's perfect.

While I'm getting my blades arranged, Inkga cleans up. When it's Julina's turn, she insists we need another guard, but I veto her position. While she washes, Inkga does my hair in fancy knots.

When Julina emerges from the other side of the dressing screen wearing her uniform, I say, "See? Nothing bad happened to me. I wasn't attacked, though I could have handled it."

"The point is you shouldn't have to handle it." She adds, "Your Majesty."

"Maybe." It's the best I can do at conceding.

"Are you ready?" Inkga asks me.

I'd rather stay here and work on my fighting skills. But I did already put on a dress. "I suppose."

The guards around my door surround me as best they can as I exit my room. When we get out of the inn, the rest of the guards are ready. It would be better if they found their rooms and cleaned up as well, but they still look travel-worn. I guess I can't control everything, but I wish things weren't so much about me, even if I understand why they are.

Opla waits for us in the middle of the road. We move forward as one body, and my entourage parts as we reach her.

"Are you ready for celebration?" she asks after a curtsy.

No. "I'm looking forward to it."

"Wonderful. The citizens are most anxious to meet with you."

We travel down the street. The farther we go, the louder it gets —the sound of a crowd having the time of their lives. There are so many people that they drift off into the distance. My guards keep close, surrounding me and Opla.

As we reach the crowd, the noise decreases until the only sound is the faint commotion of children and mothers shushing them. The crowd bows low. I call out, "Please rise."

The people get to their feet. They're still abnormally silent, making me tense and wanting to grab my daggers. I reach up to make sure my poison pouch is around my neck under my clothes. Not that either that or my blades would do me any good if the crowd attacked. Even my guards couldn't protect me from all of them.

I glance at faces as we walk by. Some are solemn, but others are eager. There's a mother pointing me out to her children. A man with a little boy on his shoulders. A young man, not much older than me, watching with eager eyes.

What must all these people think of me?

We come to a long table facing outward to the crowd, with no one behind it. Opla motions for me to go to it first. With guards in tow, I go around and stand behind the middle seat. Opla and others I'm not familiar with stand behind the seats beside me.

Should I sit? Is that what they're waiting for, or is it something else I'm unaware of? I'm about to sit when movement to the right catches my eye. I glance over, hands on the hilts of my daggers, and realize it's Inkga. I relax and take in what she's carrying.

A tray with the Mortum Tura on it. I didn't realize we brought it with us, but it makes sense. The way it makes me glow will confirm to them that I am their ruler. That I belong in my place.

Inkga holds out the tray. I take the chalice and bring it to my lips, but then I hesitate. The First Queen said the more I drank, the more powerful I'd become. The pressure of the cup is soft against my bottom lip.

I feel the First Queen's presence, faint but steady. Every eye is on me. I don't know why I can't bring myself to drink. I can't make the crowd wait any longer. I lift the chalice, drinking the sweet liquid. Once I'm done, I set it back on the tray.

The crowd watches me with widening eyes. They drop to the ground, bowing lower than they did before. Everyone at the table gets down on their knees as well.

I know what they see, even if I can't myself. I remember the time I drank it in the room with mirrors and saw myself glowing. That's what is before them now.

I take a moment to collect myself. There's much I could do with this type of power over the people. The First Queen's presence wanes until I can no longer feel it. What I want to do with the power is help the people. To make things better for them, not rule over them.

"Rise." My voice carries through the stillness despite the vast gathering.

The crowd rises. They look at me, their mouths wide with wonder. I wonder how long I'll glow for.

Opla motions her hand to me. "Citizens, meet Queen Ryn, your newest ruler. She has come to join with us in these festivities." She glances at me as if she expects me to say something.

What would be the proper words to speak at such a time? I draw on all my time spent with the ladies-in-waiting. "Thank you for meeting with me this day. I appreciate you taking time out of your day to celebrate and enjoy the good things your community has to offer."

I take a seat, and thankfully, the others at the table follow suit. Food is set in front of me first and then in front of the others. I hurry to take a bite so the others don't wait for me. The food is sweet with a hint of herbs.

Sound fills the space as people start talking again and gazes are shifted away from me. I want to relax my shoulders. Curl in on myself. Instead, I hold my form and take another bite.

Opla introduces me to others at the table, who all smile and nod politely.

The people in the crowd head to tables I didn't notice before, laden with food. They must have a lot of farms nearby that do well for so much food to be found in one place. The noise grows as chatter, laughter, and squeals of delight fill the air.

The conversation around me is more subdued; hardly anyone says anything. The evening wears on, the sun streaking bright colors across the sky as it goes down. It's then I notice an anomaly in the crowd.

The innkeeper's wife is here, staring at me. It wouldn't bother me since there are many people watching me, but she never looks away. Neither does she look happy. A chill on the back of my neck says something isn't as it should be.

I discreetly point her out to Julina, who says, "Maybe she's making sure she's ready for when you come back to the inn, but we'll keep an eye on her."

Julina whispers to a few other guards, but I'm restless. It's probably being the center of attention for this long.

The food gives way to dancing and merriment. No one asks me to join in, and though I think about it, I refrain. Last time I danced in a crowd, Daros was spotted. I doubt he would be again, but the thought holds me back.

Another thing to consider is that I can't touch anyone. This dance is a little different than in Indell. Partners are mostly apart from each other but sometimes come together to hold hands and swing in a circle. If I wanted to dance, I wouldn't have to hold anyone, but I don't want to interrupt.

"What do you think of the dancing?" Opla breaks the silence at our table.

"It's charming," I say.

"They don't often have reason to dance. I think it's good for them."

"As do I."

We talk about the city, how the farms are thriving, but the food mostly stays here, not being traded with other towns because of taxes. I didn't realize taxes for trade between cities was so bad. At some point, rulers have deiced that it's better to overcharge the people in everything, rather than trying to get them to be productive and make a better life that way. Not that we can do without taxes all together, but there needs to be some type of happy balance that works for everyone.

Opla goes back to being quiet, and the night wears on. Once darkness creeps in fully, torches are brought out to light up the area.

Finally, it's time to go back to the inn. I have much to occupy my thoughts.

CHAPTER 20

THE NIGHT AIR IS STIFLING, despite me not being under any blankets. The bed is lumpy and makes me want to sleep on the floor, but at least it's not as bad as at the last inn. It may be uneven, but it's soft. I roll over once again, trying to get comfortable. I need a fresh breeze.

I slip out of bed, bare feet rubbing against the smooth wood. I grab a dagger from under my pillow and check for my poison pouch out of habit. Though I'm only going to the window, it feels wrong to go without being prepared. I all too often remember when I first came to the palace and went to the queen's bathing rooms without weapons and was almost choked to death.

Best not repeat that.

I skim across the floor, keeping my footsteps silent. The moonlight streams in, brightening the room with its cool beam. The darkness is familiar but still eerie.

Inkga is in a makeshift bed on the couch, but Julina insisted on sleeping under the window again. I'm not certain I can open it without waking her. Depends on how light of a sleeper she is and how noisy the window is.

Back at the palace, I make sure to keep my window oiled, but here is another story. The servants should do it, and they try, but I like to keep it well-oiled myself. I plant my feet next to Julina's stomach and lean forward to open the window, hoping for some cool night air. I get the window up an inch before Julina is moving.

I block her sword with my dagger without thinking what I'm doing. I stop myself from going further and injuring her, though my muscles want to.

"Ryn?" Julina's voice is a sleepy whisper, belying the pressure of her blade against mine.

"It's me. Just wanted some fresh air."

She lowers her sword back at her side. "You scared the life out of me. I thought you were an attacker. Next time, ask me to open the window."

"I didn't want to wake you up."

"Look how well that turned out," she grumbles and then adds, sounding much more awake, "Your Majesty."

"None of that nonsense. No one who cares is around."

She sits up, stretches, and stands before opening the window. It gives a squeak. I glance at Inkga, who jumps to her feet, eyes wide.

"Sorry," Julina says. "It's just us, opening the window."

And everyone is up. Great.

She pushes the window up the rest of the way, and the window floods the room with noise. So much for sneaking around. This window is going to wake up everyone in the place. At least the guards outside my door should already be awake since they're on watch.

"Are you ready to go back to bed, Ryn?" Inkga asks.

"I'm not tired. You two sleep. I'm going to exercise." As much as I can in this room. I doubt Julina will let me escape out the window in an unfamiliar place. I could make her, but I'm not in the mood to push my status.

"I feel wide awake," she says. "How about I get us some tea?"

I shrug. "If you'd like."

"Julina, you want something?"

"No tea. Maybe a treat, if they have some."

"Sounds good. I'll be right back."

"Take one of the guards with you." Can't be too careful.

She gives me a look that says I'm being overprotective. I don't care, as long as she stays safe. She leaves the room, a mumble of voices coming from the hallway.

I get down on the floor and start doing push-ups. I do thirty, switch to crunches, and do another thirty. By the time Inkga returns, I've done several sets, and I'm hotter than I was before. I'm going to need another bath at this rate.

"I've got tea and lemonade. The woman helping me said you might like something cool, though I brought the chamomile too. There are pastries for you, Julina."

"Lemonade sounds great." I get off the floor and grab a full cup off of Inkga's tray.

Both she and Julina grab pastries. I raise the cup to my nose and smell it out of habit before taking a sip. There's a bitter taste, faint but there, and it's more than that of a lemon. I spit it out, spraying Julina and Inkga.

They stare at me, aghast.

Instead of apologizing, I say, "Poison."

Julina drops her pastry on the floor. "Do you need an antidote? Did much get in you?"

"I'm fine. I'm immune to this type." Which means it probably wasn't Daros behind the attack. Unless he's sending some type of warning. "Still didn't want to risk it. Sorry about spraying you both."

"Forget it." Inkga mops up the spill with a handkerchief.

"We need to find out who did this." Julina storms to the door and talks to the guards outside the room. She turns back to us. "Inkga, go with Piru. He'll follow with the same guards that took you to the kitchen and you can identify the woman who helped you get this."

Inkga goes, face pale but head held high.

Several more guards enter my room. I go to my stash of weapons, put on a belt on over my nightdress, and add as many blades as I can to my person in this state of dress. When I turn around, the guards are watching me, only Julina keeping her expression neutral. Everyone else looks everything from shocked to maybe a little scared.

"What? Never seen a woman with daggers before?" I spit out.

When no one speaks, Julina comes to the rescue. "Just not that many on a queen."

"Best to be prepared."

She nods.

The rest of the wait is tense, but silent.

A man's scream pierces the air. I dart toward the door, but my guards are faster.

"Let us check it out, Your Majesty," the one closest to me says.

"Hurry." The only reply I can think of. I could force my way through—they're not allowed to touch me, and it would be the perfect excuse to make it happen—but I refrain.

The scream sounds again, painful and biting.

Three of the guards storm out into the hallway. I follow after them, Julina close on my heels, telling me to come back. I ignore her. At least I let the others go ahead of me. I won't sit idly by if I can help, though.

The scream comes a third time, several doors down from mine, away from the stairs. The guards ahead of me get there and try the door knob. "Locked," one of them says.

I growl.

"Excuse me, Your Majesty." Julina digs through her pockets.

I squeeze to the side, out of her way. Others are coming out into the hall now. Carver, Inyi, and Kada stare at me with wide eyes. Before they can say anything, a guard shoos them back into their rooms.

Julina pulls a lock-picking set out of her pocket. I'm jealous. Daros always kept mine, except for certain jobs, and I never had it replaced.

It takes her a good minute to unlock the door, in which time another yell comes from the room. She pulls her sword out, nods to the other guards, and opens the door. What she sees brings a pained expression to her face, but she puts her sword in its sheath.

Confused, I press forward, and the guards move out of my way, some deeper into the room and others in the hallway.

When I see what caused the noise, my heart drops.

Nash.

More nightmares.

More pain.

An anguish I can't take away. I didn't recognize his screams due to how brutal they sounded. At least I can wake him up. And not like last time, when someone almost got hurt. I grab a pitcher of water that's sitting by the wash basin and throw it on him.

He bolts upward, chest heaving, water dripping down his face. His hands clench as his gaze darts around the room. His eyes are wild. Frantic.

My heart gives a painful twist. I want to go to him, but I can't. Not with everyone watching. I shouldn't be here, risking his life. I keep my expression neutral, voice firm. "Nash. You're at the inn, in Pulfa. You're safe."

The wild look leaves his eyes, but his fists stay clenched.

"Are you all right?" I ask.

He gives a curt nod.

"If you need anything, let one of the guards or servants know." I don't wait for an answer before heading out of the room. If I want to keep him safe, his room is the last place I should be in the middle of the night.

I go back to my quarters, trying to push Nash from my mind.

Of course, he won't go. He sits there, just as much as he sat in his bed, looking scared. Like a caged, beaten animal.

I clench my jaw.

The guards follow me in, except for a few who stay out in the hall. I move toward the window.

Julina stops me. "Please stay away from the window until we can assess the threat, Your Majesty."

"Fine." The word comes out harsher than I meant, but I don't take it back.

Several minutes later, I hear the soft thud of multiple sets of footsteps coming down the hall. Inkga enters the room, followed by the guards surrounding the innkeeper's wife. Her face is drawn into a scowl fiercer than the last one she gave me, but when she speaks, her words are cordial. "You needed me, Your Highness?"

Not how I expected my poisoner to act. "Did you help Inkga, my servant here, with getting a tray of refreshments?"

"I did."

"Did you also know that tray held poisoned lemonade?"

Her frown falls with the drop of her mouth. "Poisoned?"

"Yes. With a most deadly one. If I wasn't familiar with it, I would be dying right now."

She blanches.

"Do you have anything to do with this?" I ask.

"No. I would never harm the queen." Her voice shakes.

"What are you hiding?"

"N-nothing."

And I'm a fila, they mythical cat that doesn't exist. "It will go easier if you tell me now." I handle the dagger in my hand, running one of my fingers down its length.

"I don't know anything for certain, but..."

When she doesn't say more, I use a quiet but forceful tone. "But what?"

Her chin quivers. "I think my husband may be involved."

"Go find the innkeeper," I tell my guards.

Half of them break off and head out of the room. Julina stays close.

"Tell me everything," I say. If her husband is involved, how can she not be? And though I know appearances are deceiving—I'm proof enough of that—she was the one scowling at me while he was welcoming. What is going on?

"I knew something was up when we received word you would be using our inn during your stay. He was happy but secretive. I thought maybe he was seeing another woman." That might explain her attitude. "He snuck around a lot, coming home drunk at late hours and leaving me to tend the inn by myself. When I confronted him about it, he assured me there was no other woman and nothing was wrong. Things were about to be better than ever."

Better than ever? By poisoning me? Something doesn't add up.

"Then this morning he was more jovial than ever, singing and dancing through the inn, though customers were giving him funny looks. When I was back with the cook, I saw him thumbing a vial. I asked him what it was, and he snapped that it was nothing and hurried to put it in his pocket.

"When your servant came for refreshments, I helped her—yes —but I went into the kitchens without her. My husband was waiting. He told me he would take care of the drinks while I got some pastries. He even suggested adding lemonade to the tray since it was so hot out. I thought it was a good idea, though he's not usually so generous. I figured the crown must be paying a lot for you to stay here, and he wanted to keep you on good terms. We finished the tray, and I brought it out to your servant. When I returned to the kitchen, my husband was gone. I haven't seen him since."

Good terms, indeed.

"Is it true she went into the kitchens without you?" I ask Inkga.

"It is."

I nod at the innkeeper's wife. "You are confined to another

room, where one of my guards will watch over you until we get this sorted."

"For what it's worth, I hope you find my husband." Her scowl returns, and she goes out the door with Piru.

She must be bitter from his actions. That, or she wants to make certain the blame gets put on him and not her. He'd better be found, either way.

"Inkga, will you take a guard and round up everyone but Shillian and Carver? I would like to talk to my council members that are here. Also let Inyi go back to sleep." She'll find out soon enough. I can't deal with her fainting right now.

"I'll be back soon, Your Majesty." Inkga heads from the room, a guard slipping away with her.

It's going to be a much longer night than I anticipated.

CHAPTER 21

EVERYONE IS GATHERED around the inn's main floor. The others pushed tables and chairs around until we could all be in a circle. The guards surround us, alternating between looking in toward the circle and looking out. Nash is on my right side, but Jaku broke protocol by being on my left.

When he was awakened he was furious we didn't get him sooner, but he'll have to deal with that. I can only handle so many details at a time, unless I'm working a job. Granted, I don't do assassin jobs anymore. Sometimes I think it'd be easier than what my current work is, though.

"What's this about?" Kada asks. "I heard screaming."

"Uh, yes." I don't want to bring Nash into this any more than he already is. "Someone tried to poison my drink."

"We've interrogated the wife of the innkeeper," Julina says from behind me. "She seems to think her husband is the culprit. We have guards looking for him, and she is in custody. I have someone going to find the local guards, to see if there's somewhere we can detain her."

"Why was I not woken for this?" Jaku's voice holds a note of anger.

I jump in. "We woke you as soon as we could. It happened quickly."

"Still, I should have been notified sooner," he says, though he sounds more mollified. "We need to see what the innkeeper has to say. How soon do you think we'll find him?"

"With help from his wife, we'll hopefully be able to locate him quickly. She's giving us all the spots he's been known to frequent." Julina appears confident.

Sidle isn't as much. "Hopefully? We need more than that. I can go out and help look."

I motion for him to go with a finger. "Feel free. Anyone else?"

"I'd join, but I need to stay at your side if things continue to be dangerous," Jaku says.

I don't bother telling him I can protect myself. As true as it is, he can't seem to see it. "Inkga, relate your tale to them."

She does so. I listen for new details, but nothing stands out. When she's finished, a few questions are asked for clarification, but nothing useful. Nash is oddly silent. I want to look at him. To ask him if he's all right after that nightmare. The pull toward him is undeniable. It's like we're supposed to be together, even if the rest of the country thinks we're not.

Maybe they're right.

If it's going to cause all sorts of problems for us to be together, maybe I should stop being so open with him, even in private. Not that I want to.

I just want to be with him.

"Your Majesty?" Kada's voice pulls me out of thoughts that I shouldn't be having at a time like this.

"Repeat the question."

"Do you want us to wait up until they find him, or should we sleep on it until we have news?"

Either way, I won't be rested for tomorrow. "We can sleep on it. Feel free to go back to your rooms. I'll have someone get each of you, should any news arise."

With the meeting at a close, Kada and Inkga enter a discussion I can't hear. Nash and Jaku are silent at my sides, neither moving.

I don't move either. What's the point? Go up to my room and pretend to sleep? I suppose I could get more training in. It's a good idea. I need to stay at my prime, and it's better than wasting my time here, doing nothing.

My ladies-in-waiting come to mind before I stand. What would they do in this circumstance? If I stand, everyone else will have to as well. Inkga and Kada are still in a conversation. I don't wish everyone to make a big deal of me.

I let out the smallest of sighs. It doesn't matter what I want. Everything about me is a big deal now. How I live. Stupid ideas about how I should die. I should have run to another country instead of becoming queen. But then I wouldn't know Nash or Inkga, and I wouldn't be able to help the people.

It's a conundrum.

I'm about to give up and stand anyway when a guard enters the room. "We've found him," he says.

"Good. Bring him in for questioning," I say.

The guard nods and leaves the room. A moment later he reenters and steps to the side. A group of guards including Sidle come in, the innkeeper in the midst of them, hands tied behind his back and a guard holding each of his arms. They force him forward and onto his knees before me. The innkeeper jerks, but the men hold him steady.

"I'm going to ask you questions. You're going to answer," I say.

He sneers, the look not nearly as good on him as his previous cheer.

"Did you poison my drink?" I ask.

He scowls instead of replying.

I take out my dagger and brush my fingers against the flat metal. "I'm going to ask again. Did you poison my drink?"

His lips quiver, like he's fighting himself about whether or not to speak.

I get off my chair, and everyone in the room jumps to their feet. I ignore them as I crouch down and in his face. "I'm sure you've heard rumors of who I am." I lower my voice. "Should we see if those rumors are true?"

He visibly swallows. "I poisoned all the drinks on the tray sent up to you."

Better. "Were you working alone or with someone?"

"With someone."

"Who?"

"I don't know. I never saw him." His voice shakes. "He wore a hood when we met."

Daros? I swallow back my bile. "What did he tell you?"

"He said that if I poisoned you when you came, he would reward me. Paid me a hundred gold coins in advance and said there was more coming if I did what he said. He gave me the poison. I figured I could run and hide and then come back for my wife later."

I snort. "But you didn't plan on being caught."

"You didn't care about killing your ruler?" Jaku asks.

The innkeeper gives a half shrug—about all he can manage while tied up.

"Was your wife involved?" Sidle asks.

"No. She knew nothing."

Not that he's honest. It's difficult to say whether or not he is, but I'm inclined to believe him. "How did the man find you?"

"I don't know how. He came into my inn one day and asked to speak with me. It was late at night when no one else was around."

"Did you notice anything else about him? Anything at all?"

He shakes his head. "It was dark and his cloak was dark."

I've heard enough. "Send him to Opla. She can decide what his fate will be."

The guards yank him to his feet and haul him out of the room while I take my seat. The remaining guards make their way to the outside of the circle, and the council members present retake their chairs.

"Who do you think is behind the plot?" Kada asks.

I wish she wouldn't have. Ever since the innkeeper mentioned working with a cloaked man I've been trying not to think of it, but could it be Daros?

Nash asks just that.

"It's uncertain." I don't want to give too much away, but they have a right to know. "Daros knows I'm immune to the poison the innkeeper tried to administer, but he could be toying with me." It wouldn't be the first time.

"So we have an unknown accomplice still roaming the streets?" Jaku leans forward. "We should go back to the palace. It's not safe here for you."

"It's not safe back there, either. I am in danger wherever I go." Besides, after the city's reception—well, most of the people with their kindness—I need to see the others around the country. I need to show them I care about them and their problems.

"I believe Her Majesty to be correct," Sidle says. "She's going to be in danger, no matter where we take her."

"But we can guard her more securely at the palace," Jaku insists.

Sidle looks at me before turning his gaze back to Jaku. "We can guard her securely here. We have enough manpower for it. We should get a taster for her food, but otherwise, I don't think there's anything an attacker can do to her. If they could, they would have done more than a half-hearted poison attempt."

Jaku opens his mouth, but I beat him to it. "I agree with Sidle. We will continue with our plan, though I don't need a taster. I'm adept enough at poisons on my own."

"If we're going to stay, I'm going to insist on a taster," Jaku says.

"I won't have that person's death on my conscience, should they fail."

"And I won't have your death on my conscience, should you fail." Jaku's words are more heated than I've heard them before.

I didn't know my life meant so much to him. "Very well. But make certain you find someone well-trained. I don't want to have someone dying because of me." I have enough blood on my hands.

"Consider it done."

Now to get out of this town, where death lingers, and hope Opla can take care of the mess we leave behind without too much trouble.

CHAPTER 22

DESPITE OUR LEAVING BEHIND AT LEAST one criminal, Opla insists we continue on with our journey. The people wave their good-byes as I get into the carriage. The door is closed behind me, and I wave out the window.

We ride long and fast. We stop to change when we're close enough not to make too many wrinkles in our clothes, but far enough the people can't see me yet. A fresh dress for me and Inyi. Inkga helps tidy up our hair, and we're off again.

I worry about what we left behind, for Opla to deal with—Daros or some other foe. It's not going to go easy, either way, but I hope it's someone else. Without any clues as to where that person might be, I'd rather deal with a stranger than Daros.

Why would Daros toy with me like that? What could he possibly gain? Not knowing is giving me a headache.

"Are you all right, Your Highness?" Inyi asks across from me.

"Fine." As fine as one can be, with either a sadistic madman toying with her or someone wanting her dead.

"Good, because we're almost there."

It's a lovely stop, with citizens who are a mix of happy and frustrated with me. They wear drab colors that either don't match their lovely, bright-smiling faces or perfectly match their sour expressions.

I know I can't please everyone, but it'd be nice to, anyway. The town doesn't have much for me to do. It's small and still growing. I make plans to help them develop their refuse system, so the streets are cleaner and there are more jobs available.

After a couple days of riding in the carriage and watching for signs of Daros, we come to another stop that has more cheerful people than not. I smile at a girl about my age. She grins back, and I can't help feeling a connection to her. We probably have nothing in common. It's doubtful that she's an assassin, and she's definitely not the queen. But we both seem to care for Valcora. It's enough that I wish I could stop and talk to her.

There are a lot of people I wish I could stop and speak with. They are interesting, with their bright eyes and colorful jewelry made of stones and beads. I want to learn their stories, but there isn't time for more than cursory talk.

I get more in depth with the leaders, but I only have a couple of days to spend with even them. I want to get a better idea of what they are like. How they are helping the country, and what I can do to assist.

There is a town named Ilsar we stop at where I make jobs to make better streets. Theirs are small, dirt roads that kick up a lot of dust. In a growing town, they need something better. I wish it was mason work, and I could give Carver work, but it's a stone-layer's job. There are many men willing and eager to get started. They seem grateful for the work and are lined up waving and smiling as I leave.

When we reach the next town, Dunin, it's almost dark, the sun's rays goldening the sky. Inkga gives me an encouraging smile. I return it, pretending everything is fine when all I want to do is watch for Daros. A dull ache is behind my eyes, growing by the moment. I'll have to grin and bear through it, though. There's supposed to be another celebration tonight.

We pass houses that are more like the shacks the Poruah live in, only they remain that way all through the town. Nothing is big or fancy. Like the last town, there are no bright colors when we go by the crowds. Browns and grays dominate their wardrobe.

I push thoughts of Daros and my headache aside in favor of thinking about the country. The people need something more than the last town; that much is evident. But what can I give them? How can I help them? What do they need? There must be something I can do.

We roll to a stop in front of a crowd. A servant opens the door to my carriage, and I glide out. The servant yells loud enough for all to hear, "Presenting Queen Ryn."

The crowd cheers, a deafening sound for how much smaller their numbers are than the last town. I smile and wave, even as the noise makes my head pound.

Off to the side and toward the back, there's a group that's not cheering. Not that I demand praise, but these people look down-right ornery. What did I do to offend them? It's probably my being an assassin who dithers over laws. It's enough to make me upset. Why not them as well?

I suppress a sigh and lower my hand. A man walks up to me and bows. "May I present our esteemed leader, Fulla of Trentin?"

The crowd parts, no longer cheering. A woman moves between them, coming at me with a grin and clothes fancier than the ones I'm wearing. Her yellow-green dress and its many flounces appear to be made of silk. The people are careful to stay far away from her. Once she's several feet from me, she gives the smallest curtsy necessary. "Greetings, Your Majesty. We are over-joyed by your presence."

"Thank you for your people's warm welcome." Because hers certainly wasn't.

"You and your guests will be staying with me. My man will

show you the way when you are ready. Feel free to linger with the townsfolk as long as you like, and then you will have dinner with me."

Not a celebration? Maybe she thinks a dinner with her is celebration enough. Not that I have to have one, but every town has given one so far. I nod and smile. She gives her excuses and departs. As soon as she's gone, I hear a cry that grows nearer. I turn to find Shillian coming at me, tears in her eyes.

"I heard what happened. Why didn't you tell me sooner? I can't believe someone tried to kill you, and you don't want to return to the palace. I want my little girl safe."

I glance at the crowd watching us. Some are close enough to hear our words. I give them a smile and a wave before turning my attention back to her.

Carver comes up behind her and puts a hand on her shoulder. "We don't want to frighten everyone off," he says in a low voice.

I give him a genuine smile. I appreciate the effort he's going to. "I'm safe. We're taking extra precautions. Everything will be fine, but I need to be with the people now. Why don't you both go on ahead and get ready for dinner? I'd be happy if you would join me there."

"We would love to," Carver says, guiding his wife the way Fulla went.

For a moment, she looks as if she's going to protest, but then she goes along with him smoothly.

There's a tingling at my back. I turn, ready to draw my daggers.

"It's just me," Nash whispers.

Great. I overreacted in front of a crowd. As if they don't already have reason to fear the Shadow Wraith.

"Do you want to go out among the people or to follow Fulla?"

What I want is some alone time to talk to him. And to kiss his face off. "Let me go among the people."

He motions to the guards, and they reform into two lines, one on each side of me in the middle of the crowd, nothing between them but hard packed dirt. Nash holds a hand out in front of him, indicating I should go first.

I walk forward, anxious. Whether it's to meet the people or because of them, I'm uncertain. I step through the pathway and grin first at one side, and then the other. Some people smile back while others scowl. I pretend they're all smiling.

A little girl waves wildly at me, eyes wide. I stop and bend down to her level. "What's your name?"

"Wapli."

"How old are you?"

"This many." She holds up a hand with all her fingers extended.

"Five years old is a big girl."

"I always wanted to meet the queen."

I grin at her. "And I always wanted to meet a five-year-old girl named Wapli."

Her eyes grow wider. "Really?"

"Yes."

"Wow."

Nash bends down beside me and holds out a gold coin. "For the beautiful girl named Wapli, who the queen always wanted to meet."

"For me?"

"It is."

She takes the coin from Nash. "Thank you, sir. Thank you both."

She holds the coin close to her. I stand up straight and walk on. When I make eye contact with Nash, he winks. A flutter goes through my stomach. It takes great strength not to take hold of his hand. Instead, I wave to the crowd.

I stop and talk to a few more townsfolk, but none as interesting as the little girl. Nash passes out more coins. The crowd is eager to get to him, and hold their coins with a reverence I've never seen. Judging by their thinness and drab clothing, they need them.

The part of the crowd that looked on with scowls before doesn't try to approach. They stay far away, watching. The guards walk with me, maintaining the alley. The houses on both sides of us are bigger than before but dilapidated.

THERE'S one house ahead that stands out from all the others. It's a mini palace in its own right. It towers over the rest of the buildings. A yellow wall surrounds it, making it so you have to go through the front gate. The group avoids that gate, only following us until we near it.

My guards cluster around me and Nash as we go through the gate, some leading the way and some staying behind. The great building looms over us, not nearly as big as the palace but so much bigger than everything else here that it's disarming.

A servant shows us in and to our own rooms. I force myself not to make eye contact with Nash when we part. Inkga helps me freshen up for dinner, and I soon find myself waiting beside Inyi, Shillian, and Carver. The host has not yet arrived, which surprises me since she left before us. That, and everyone usually makes the world revolve around me. Not that I like it, but the difference is noticeable.

I turn to Shillian and Carver after the others bow at my entrance and make small talk. "How are you enjoying the trip so far?"

"It was lovely until someone tried to kill you," Shillian says. "How often does this happen?"

More than I care to admit. At least to her. "Often enough we have precautions in place. I'm apt at keeping myself from harm."

"How do you do it?" Carver asks.

I shrug. "I had a lot of training growing up. Where Daros was a horrid father figure, he was a great example of self-preservation."

"I'm sorry we left you with a madman, but I'm glad you were able to learn the things you needed to keep yourself alive."

I wave away his concern, though it stirs something inside me. "It is what it is. Being immune to most poisons and keeping up the skills that will protect my life is a good trade off." Now anyway. Before, I would have given anything to grow up differently, but it's made me the person I am.

"It's good you're able to protect yourself. I wish I'd made a better judgment call," Shillian says.

I want to reach out to her. To comfort her. But I can't risk her life. Family should be allowed to touch, but no. Not even that is allowed. According to the rules, they might tarnish me with their common nature. It's daft.

"Welcome to my home," Fulla says from behind me.

I turn to find her dressed in an even more elaborate dress. It's green with lace flounces and more ruffles than I've seen on one dress. Her wide skirt is split to reveal a pink underskirt with even more ruffles.

She walks straight to me. "I hope you find everything to your liking."

"It rivals the palace."

She grins.

It wasn't a compliment.

"Dinner is served," a servant says from the door.

Fulla moves toward the dining room and then stops herself with a giggle. "Forgive me. You first, of course."

I'd rather not put my back to everyone, but I'll have to trust my guards and daggers. I move forward, ready to turn and attack should things come to it. I am directed to the head of the table, and Fulla takes the place across from me. Members of my party sit between us—Nash at her side, Inyi and Sidle by me.

The first course is brought out—a plate of light, fluffy biscuits, butter, and jam. Not something I'd normally have for the first course, but Fulla must like it.

As I butter my biscuit, Sidle asks, "Have you any plans to make visits outside the country?"

I hadn't thought about it. "Not at this time. Though perhaps it would be good to do so in the future."

He nods. "It's difficult to travel abroad anyway, and potentially unsafe, depending on where you go."

"I'm not sure we should share our resources outside of Valcora," Inyi says, surprising me.

"Why not?" I ask.

"They are barbarians. Savages, who want our gems and precious stones."

"I heard Torhun was run by a person who was more beast than man, but I didn't know the same held true to other countries." Which is about all I know. I wish I knew more, but I need to get my country in order before focusing on others.

"They are dangerous," Sidle says. "We should be grateful the mountains are so hard to traverse."

"Indeed." Fulla's voice crosses the table with its vivacity. "We don't talk of such things during dinner."

I want to glare at her, but I restrain myself. "What should we discuss?"

"Anything fine and grand. We like to keep topics over dinner appetizing."

The food would be more appetizing if I could throw my daggers at her hideous dress. What is it about this woman that grates me so? "What would you like to converse about?"

"I'm dying to know—how did you decide to take the Mortum Tura? It's a far stretch from being an assassin." She smiles, but there's an edge to it.

My thoughts go dark, as I'm pulled back to that time. I've changed much since. I don't want to ever go back there, and I'll be daggered if she pulls me down. "Doesn't every little girl want to be a queen?"

"Not when it means the possibility of death." She takes a dainty bite.

"Those of us who have been with Queen Ryn have seen she has no fear, even for death," Nash says.

I refrain from sending him a grateful smile. If only he knew how often I fear things... I don't show it to many.

Fulla lifts an eyebrow, as if challenging me to say something for myself. Little does she know a challenge like that is no challenge at all.

I take a bite of the salad that was just brought out and placed in front of me, the oil and vinegar tangy.

When I don't respond, she goes on to other topics. I try not to look relieved, but I am very much so.

After she's been talking a while, I catch Nash's gaze. His expression is so neutral, I'm dying to know what he's thinking. But I can't ask. Not now. Not here. I may not get another chance to speak with him until we're back at the palace. I sigh.

"Are you all right?" Inyi whispers.

"Fine. Thinking of my bed back home." Home. Is that what the palace has become? I've lived in a house before, but I never had a place I could call *home*. The palace is such a strange place to think of as such, but I'm happy to, anyway.

"I don't blame you. I'd rather have my own bed as well."

The rest of the meal continues with us talking of trivialities. No one makes a misstep, though Fulla keeps a close eye on me. I wonder what she's thinking.

When we finish dinner, Fulla says we can go to our rooms because we probably need the rest. Another urge to throw my dagger at her comes to me. The woman is far too bossy. I've had more than enough for a lifetime.

Still, it's a good excuse to get away from her, so Inkga, Julina, and I converge in our assigned room.

"It's not often we have a dinner like that," Inkga says.

"No. It isn't." I let her unpin my hair.

"One might think Fulla wanted you to be disgraced in front of everyone."

"That's the feeling I got, too. It wouldn't have been hard to do a few months ago."

"But you've grown a lot since."

One can only hope.

CHAPTER 23

"I'M GOING TO TAKE A WALK," I announce to Inkga and Julina.

"I'll come with you," Julina replies.

"Can you be quiet, walking on a roof?"

Inkga gives me a funny look.

"She does it all the time," Julina tells her. "She thinks she's sneaky, but one of us always follows her."

"I know that," I say. "If I wanted to lose you, I could."

She focuses her gaze on me, serious. "I believe it."

"What makes you want to climb on the roof here?" Inkga asks.

"A hunch." Or my dislike for Fulla is clouding my judgment. Either way, I want to get out, into the cool night air. It will be a welcome relief from the heat of the day.

"You're going to do it no matter what I say, so I might as well go with you," Julina says.

Good. "Let me change, and we'll leave."

I exchange my dress for black pants and a shirt. I consider letting my hair down to cover my neck but decide against it. If it's pinned back, it won't get in my way. I re-stash all my daggers on me. "I'm ready."

Julina nods. "We should tell the other guards we're leaving."

"Inkga can tell them where we went if we don't come back. I want as little attention on us as possible."

"I can do that," Inkga says.

"I don't like the sound of this," Julina says. "It seems like you're about to do something dangerous."

I grin and head for the window. She sighs and follows. I open the window, and four guards look at me from outside.

"Can we help you, Your Highness?" the nearest one asks.

"Just going for a stroll. Julina's coming with me."

"Very good."

I swing out of the window, careful not to kick anyone in the head. The stone walls of the outer structure are warm beneath my touch, but the night air is cooling them off.

I begin my ascent, checking back to make sure Julina is making it. She climbs up right behind me. I shimmy up the wall until we reach the third story and, finally, the roof. I ease myself onto it, careful not to make any noise. Julina is just as silent. When she stands beside me, I give an approving nod.

"What are we looking for?" she whispers.

"Fulla's room."

"Any idea where that will be?"

Knowing her, somewhere grand, not that we can tell that from the roof. "Let's look on the other side. Can we spread out?"

"I'd rather stick by you, especially since we're spying on the ruler of this city."

I should have known. At least she didn't protest my coming.

I cross to the other side of the roof, careful to keep my footsteps stealthy. The back of the mansion is similar to the front, though instead of a grand entrance, there's an exit that leads to the gardens. It's too dark to make much out, but I can tell there's vegetation.

"There." I follow where Julina is pointing.

A balcony on the other side, middle floor, is lit up from the room inside. The light flickers but is bright enough it must be produced by many candles. It's too hot for such things, but Fulla must not care.

"That has to be it." I skirt toward the empty balcony, going more slowly than before to ensure no noise is heard.

Julina doesn't have as much luck. A crunching sound comes from behind me. I glare at her. She has the smarts to look sheepish. I make a motion for her to stop there, but she shakes her head. Stubborn woman.

I ignore her, hoping she doesn't make more noise that will give us away. It doesn't take long to reach the side of the mansion we need despite the size of the roof. It's easier without all the hallways to traverse.

Making certain there's no one on the balcony, I skimmer down the wall and end up on the outside of the railing. Moments later, Julina is beside me with a soft *plop* of a landing.

"Did you hear that?" Fulla's voice drifts out from the open doors.

"No," says a man.

"I heard something outside. Please check."

I grip the floor and swing down below the balcony with my hands hanging onto the balcony floor so I can't be seen. Julina follows suit. I hear footsteps coming onto the balcony.

"I don't see anything," the man says.

"Are you certain?" Fulla's voice comes nearer. "I could have sworn I heard something."

I glare at Julina. She doesn't look at me. Her eyes are closed, her arms shaking.

Sure, my arms burn, but I can handle this. I'm not sure she will last much longer. Or perhaps that's how she lasts.

"There's nothing here," the man says.

"Hmm." Fulla's voice is quite close now. "It is a nice night out. Better than that stifling room. Even worse was dinner. You should have heard the conversations the queen tried to make. Obscene."

I make a face.

"Should we talk out here or in your room?"

"Out here is so lovely. Let's stay."

I nudge Julina with my foot. She finally glances at me. I tilt my head toward the wall. She nods. As Julina moves toward the wall, Fulla says, "I don't know what we're going to do about her presence here."

"She shouldn't stay long. She and her party are set to continue on their country tour the day after tomorrow."

Julina is on the wall now, propping herself up with her feet as she flattens herself and moves under the balcony.

"That is so, but if she discovers what I've done, she'll surely change things." Fulla whines. "Queen Deedra was much more understanding than the reports we've heard of this Ryn girl."

I seethe under being called *girl*. Reminds me too much of Daros. And what will I want to change? If Deedra liked it, it might have been hard for the people. My arms burn, the weight of my body held fully on them starting to take its toll. I shift over one hand at a time, heading toward the wall.

"Queen Deedra was the one who suggested you tax the city if you weren't getting enough money from the crown. Of course she was all right with it. You don't think the new queen will approve?"

No, I won't. My arms tremble with more than the strain of holding myself up.

"I don't know. The reports don't sound good."

I get to the wall and press my feet up against it, finding a purchase. I shift my hands so I hold on to it, as well. Though the stones don't stick out as far as my fingers and toes would like, it's much easier to support my weight with four limbs instead of two.

I'm right next to Julina, though if someone were to look over the edge, they would only see me and not her since she's fully under the balcony.

"Things will be fine," the man says. "We need to wine and dine her while she's here, and all will be well."

"If you say so."

"Come here, love." There's a rustling sound. "You worry too much."

The response is so low, I can't make it out. It's quiet.

Julina sneezes.

"What was that?" Fulla asks.

Julina is already on the move, making room for me, but there won't be time judging by the footsteps coming closer. I swing down and make it under the balcony. The question is, was I quick enough?

I pause and hold my breath as I cling to the wall.

"There's nothing here," the man says.

"No, I heard something. I know I did." Fulla sounds frustrated.

"I heard it too, but there's nothing here. We'd best go inside."

The footsteps fade, and so do Fulla's complaints. I give a relieved sigh when I hear a door close. And now they're back in their stuffy room. We can get back to ours, but I want to stay outside longer. There are things I need to think about, and it's easier to do that out here.

I turn to make sure Julina is following me before I snake forward, slithering up the wall. It takes Julina a lot longer to make her way up, but she gets there in the end.

Without a word, we traverse back toward our side of the building. Over my window, she motions for me to go first.

Instead, I sit on the ledge. "I'd rather stay outside."

"Fine." She plops down beside me.

What were that man and Fulla talking about? Taxes that are doing what to my people? I need to talk to those who live here. Need to see what they think—hear for myself what their taxes are like.

Judging from the town, they are mostly Poruah. They should be paying minimal taxes, and to the country only, but who knows what they're going through if Deedra arranged something else with Fulla?

As far as I understand it, the city should have plenty of money from the crown. I don't know why we'd hoard away what belongs to them. Besides, the tax collectors in each city bring it to the local ruler's Head of Treasury, and they take out what is owed the city before sending it on to the capital.

I wish Nash was here to talk this out with.

I could go to sleep and talk it over with the first queen.

"Forgive me if it's not my place," Julina whispers, "but I think that there's something shady going on we need to investigate."

I look at her in surprise. "You are willing to help me with that?"

"Of course. I care about these people too. It's clear Fulla doesn't want you finding out about the taxes. If you can't get away tomorrow, I could look into this for you."

"What if someone stops you?"

"It'll be like when I tried to stop you from coming up here."

I laugh, low and quiet.

"Queen Ryn, is that you?" a female voice comes from below.

I glance down to find Inkga staring up at me. "What do you need?"

"We've got trouble."

"What trouble?"

Before she can answer, she's yanked inside. I draw a knife and ready myself to climb down when Jaku pokes his head out of the window.

"You left without telling me," he says, voice like a blade of its own finding a target.

Daggered. I slide my dagger back into its sheathe. Might as well get this over with.

I climb down and swing into my room. Julina slides in moments after me.

"I had Julina with me," I tell Jaku, who's staring me down, his hands on his hips. "I was perfectly safe the whole time." Except maybe when Julina sneezed, but I'm not going there.

"You are in danger every moment, from attacks on all sides.

This isn't like back at the palace, where we can follow you on the roof and guarantee your safety. You need more than one guard with you at all times." He runs a hand through his graying hair.

Wait. Graying? When did that happen? It snuck up on me. I can't help but wonder if I caused some—or all—of it. "I'm better protected than you know. Besides, we found out vital information."

"Of course you did." He focuses in on Julina. "You should be ashamed of yourself, letting her go like that. What if there were assassins on the roof?"

I roll my eyes. "She didn't have a choice. I was determined to go. She should be praised for managing to stick by my side all the time." Even if she doesn't know how to hold in a sneeze.

"It's fine, Your Majesty," Julina says. "I'll take whatever punishment he thinks I deserve."

"It's *Ryn*. I'll start doling out punishments for those who can't remember that when others aren't around."

Jaku looks at the ceiling. "Ryn, you have to be more careful."

"I knew everything was going to be fine." All right—I hoped. But it turned out well.

He gives an exasperated sigh. "I don't know what to do with the two of you. Consider this a warning that I'll be keeping a closer eye on you both. What did you find out?"

I contemplate telling him, but the more who know about it, the more likely word is to get out. Not that I don't trust him; he could even help. If I can trust anyone, it's the people in this room. "We overheard Fulla talking to a man. She was saying something about Queen Deedra telling her to tax the city if she wasn't getting enough from the crown. They're trying to hide it from me."

"I'm going to investigate tomorrow while they try to distract Ryn," Julina says.

Inkga shakes her head. "If they're hiding it from you, it can't be good."

"Right," Jaku says. "Julina, take two more guards with you when you go, and dress like the locals do if you can get a hold of some clothes."

"Will do, sir."

"I'll see you in the morning. And Julina? Be careful."

"I will."

"Night," I chirp.

He shakes his head and goes out the door.

Inkga turns to us. "How was it?"

"You should see her in action," Julina says. "I've seen her with a dagger—which is amazing by itself—but sneaking around, she's like a shadow."

I look at the carpet, so they won't see me blush. I wasn't called *Shadow Wraith* for nothing. "I wasn't that great. Though things would have gone better if someone hadn't sneezed."

"You sneezed?" Inkga asks Julina.

She has the decency to look embarrassed. "I couldn't help it. The sneeze came from nowhere."

"It's all right," I say. "No harm was done."

"Do you think you can find out what's going on with the taxes by talking to the citizens?" Inkga asks Julina.

"I hope so."

So do I because we have no other leads.

CHAPTER 24

As EXPECTED, Fulla takes up all my time. Starting from breakfast and all the way to dinner, she has something for me to do. Tour the mini palace. Listen to a musical. Enjoy refreshments. Talk. Talk some more. Talk even more. About the most inane things, too. It's like she's trying to kill me with boredom.

I smile through it all, glad I have my group members by my side. The person who spends the most time with Fulla is Shillian. They have the same tastes, maybe? Or perhaps Shillian is trying to get on her good side for me.

Carver approaches me. "It was a good dinner."

"The food was wonderful." All I can say while remaining honest.

"Your mother enjoys talking with other women she thinks can help."

Is it that obvious I'm watching Shillian? "Help with what?"

"With paving the way for those she cares about."

So my second guess was correct.

"She spent a lot of time trying to help me find work every time I lost my job," he says.

I want to ask him why he lost his job so much, but Inyi is in the background, reminding me to mind my manners. Instead, I say, "I'm glad she was able to help."

He gives a sad smile. "She tried, anyway."

"But didn't always succeed?"

"No."

I wonder why it's been so hard. I'm not certain it's proper to ask in this situation.

It's getting late. Is Julina back yet? I'm anxious to check, but I don't want to be an ungrateful guest. Not that the host has paid much attention to me the last half-hour or so. She must think it's late enough that I won't wander outside among the people. Shows how much she knows about me.

Night is my friend.

Shillian ends her conversation with Fulla and prances over to me and Carver. "Such a nice lady. Maybe you'd want to invite her to the palace sometime."

I exchange a glance with Carver. A smile tweaks the corner of his lips. I understand him more than I do her right now.

"We'll see," is all I can commit to. If Fulla is doing what I think, she will indeed be coming to the palace. To visit the dungeons. "I think it's time I retired."

"But it's still early, darling," Shillian says.

I give her an affectionate smile. It's nice to have someone want to spend time with me. "It's all right. I'll see you in the morning."

"Very well. Have a good evening, darling."

"Goodnight... Mother. Father." I nod at them both, wondering why my tongue called them that.

I'm still pondering it as I head toward the door. I plan on leaving straight away but stop when I see Nash talking to Fulla. I miss him. As much as I don't want to be around her, I need to be around him. Even if it's not the kind of closeness I desire.

I make my way to them, everyone giving me a wide berth. They stop talking as I join them, each curtsying or bowing to me.

I say, "I came to thank you for this day. It's been... memorable. I'm heading to my room now."

"Of course," Fulla says. "We want you to get your beauty rest before you have to leave in the morning."

I give her what I hope looks like a genuine smile, but it feels tight. "Thank you. I will see you at breakfast. Nash, if you're done speaking with Fulla, I'd like a word with you."

"Certainly, Your Majesty." He gives his regards to Fulla, and we head toward the door together. Jaku falls in line behind us, which makes sense but isn't what I was hoping for. I want alone time with Nash.

To feel his lips.

To touch his hand.

To be in his embrace.

Oh, well. Inkga will be back at the room, anyway.

"I didn't think I'd ever get out of talking with her," Nash says. "That woman grates on one's nerves."

"I thought I was the only one who felt that way," I say.

"Not by a long shot," Jaku adds from behind us.

I snicker.

As we make our way through the hallways, my hand itches to hold Nash's. I take it in my other one and clasp them tight. The urge to be with him is stronger than ever. I want to ask how he's doing. If the nightmares are bothering him while we're here. What he's doing to keep from waking the household.

From the dark circles under his eyes, he isn't sleeping much. Maybe he's avoiding it so he doesn't wake the household again. I yearn to comfort him. To give him some measure of the peace I've found from my nightmares.

Not that the First Queen's dreams are perfect, but they're easier to deal with than a nightmare.

We arrive at my rooms, where a servant opens the door for us. I walk in first, and Julina stops her pacing when she sees me.

We're all silent until everyone is in the room and the door is closed. As soon as the room is secure, I ask, "What did you find out?"

"It's worse than I feared," she says. "Everyone I've talked to said she's gathering a fifty percent tax on top of the one for the country."

I take a step back. "Fifty percent?"

"It's true. That's why the people are in such poverty. Sounds like she's been doing it for a while."

"She can't do that. Can she?" I turn to Nash and Jaku.

Jaku shrugs. "I wish I knew."

Where's Timit when I need him? Huh. Never thought I'd think that. "Nash? Do you know?"

"No. But it's safe to assume it's against the law or at least shady if she's hiding it from you."

"Forgive me, Ryn, but I think I might." Inkga sits in the corner of the room, sketching something on paper. Probably a new outfit design.

"What do you know and how?"

"I helped serve Queen Deedra before she passed."

Before I killed her, that is.

Inkga continues. "I heard some conversations she had. I didn't think much of them at the time, because we weren't supposed to think. Things are different now, though. It is a law that cities can't charge taxes, but Queen Deedra gave Fulla permission to charge what she wanted. The two were close friends, and Deedra wanted Fulla to enjoy the comforts of life."

Maybe I shouldn't feel bad about killing Deedra.

"How did I not know this?" Nash asks. "I've been learning about the laws."

"I have as well," I say. "There are so many, it's hard to keep track of them. Thank you, Inkga, for sharing. I don't think we should wait until morning to deal with this."

Jaku says, "Definitely not. Julina, please round up all the guards. We're going to pay Fulla a visit."

It doesn't take long to gather most of the guard since they're already protecting me. As soon as we're ready, we make our way across the long building to the room we were gathered in, which is now empty.

We head to her rooms next. We twist through the halls. I wish we were using the roof. It was much simpler that way.

Jaku knocks on her door. I'm in the middle of the guards, standing on my tiptoes so I can barely see. Nash is beside me.

"Just a moment," a voice calls through the door. A minute later, the door opens. The servant standing there raises her eyebrows.

Jaku doesn't give her a chance to speak. He barrels into the room. As soon as the guards in front of me go forward, I hurry after them, almost tripping on their heels.

"Move," I say and press forward.

Guards rush to get out of my way. That's better. Now I can see. Only I don't like what I see. Mother gives me a quizzical look as she stands next to Fulla, whose eyes are narrowed.

"What's going on?" Mother asks.

"We need to take care of something," I say. "Mother, will you please join me over here?"

"All right." She sounds confused but takes a step forward.

Before she can move any closer, Fulla grabs her by the arm and jerks her back. "Don't come any closer."

From a hidden pocket in her skirt, Fulla pulls out a stiletto and presses the tip of the blade against Mother's neck.

"No one move," I shout.

What have I done? Put another person I care about in danger.

Is this all I'm good for?

Despair fills me.

I shove it aside. There'll be time for that later. "What do you want, Fulla?"

"I want your guarantee that you aren't going to do anything to me. That you're going to leave things as they are and you'll get on your way, never to contact me or my people again. We'll continue to send taxes, but that's all. Otherwise, you'll leave us alone."

I sigh, as if contemplating it. I don't want to give away my true thoughts. "If I do this, you'll let her go?"

"I will."

"Fine, but you have to give her over to me."

"I have your word?"

"Yes."

She smirks. "Then you can have her."

Fulla pushes Mother forward, and Mother stumbles. I reach out to grab her but stop myself at the last moment. It's a lonely world not being able to touch anyone.

She staggers to her feet and regains her footing. I hesitate a moment. Something in me wants to hold back, but the biggest part of me wants to do this. Once Mother is among the guards, I stalk my way to Fulla. The smirk on her face flees, leaving a worried gaze. "What are you doing?"

"No one threatens my family."

"But you gave your word." Her voice quavers.

"I lied."

I lift my fist and punch her in the nose.

CHAPTER 25

FULLA IS HEADED BACK to the palace, where she'll find out what the dungeons are like. Unless the council decides to kill her for my coming in contact with her. I think it could be glossed over, but we'll see what they do. I won't let myself feel bad if they decide to execute her. There's no telling how many starved to death under her rule.

A small group of guards are escorting her and will join up with us when finished. The man who was conspiring with her is going to the palace dungeons as well.

Morning dawns, bright and early. Mother flutters around my room, helping Inkga pack the last of my things, though Inkga insisted she didn't need any help.

"I still say you didn't need to punch her," Mother says.

I want to make a snide remark about being raised by a man who did things much crueler than a simple punch, but refrain. She may be my mother, but she's not perfect.

"We're all done here," Inkga says. "I'll get some servants to carry the trunks."

"Thank you, Inkga." The words are getting easier to say.

"No problem." She heads out the door.

"Shall we?" Julina asks.

"Might as well." I follow where Inkga went, though by the time I get out in the hall, she is gone. Plenty of guards mill about, surrounding me and Mother as we go.

"I never thanked you properly for saving my life," she says to me.

"It was nothing."

"No. It was something. I've never had anyone take care of me like that before. It means a lot."

My heart gives a little squeeze. "You wouldn't have been in that situation if it wasn't for me. It was the least I could do, to get you out of it."

She puts a hand to her throat as we near the main entrance. "I've never had a knife held up to my throat. It was terrifying, but Fulla's action, not yours."

I don't correct her on the stiletto. "She wouldn't have had the chance to do that had I been more prepared."

Mother stops, making the group around us come to a halt. She waits to speak until I face her. "You can't be prepared for everything."

She turns back toward the gathered crowd and makes her way through the guard. She's right, but I wish it was different. I'm still staring after her when Julina says, "Are you ready, Your Majesty?"

I finally have a name. I wish everyone would use it all the time, even if it's not proper. "Let's go."

As we did when we first arrived in Trentin, the guards line both my sides, protecting me and creating an alleyway through the gathered crowd. I wave at them and smile, my mind on the words my mother said.

She's right. I can't prepare for everything. I can try my hardest, though.

I see a man standing with a woman and little boy. His family? I wish Nash was here to give them a coin, but he went ahead to make sure everything was taken care of.

The family is dressed in brown clothes, thin from so many washings or wearings. Their cheeks are gaunt and their eyes hungry, though there's a sparkle in them that surprises me.

The man speaks before I can say anything. "Your Majesty, it is an honor to speak with you. When we heard you were changing the taxes so much, we worried, though the end result was lower taxes to our benefit. We shouldn't have worried. Thank you for restoring our town."

His words makes the back of my eyes burn. "I wish I could do more." But I can. "I will make sure your new leader is a good person, and that once Fulla's things are sold, the profits are spread evenly to all tax payers. What can't be sold will be given away. You will have your city back."

A shout of joy goes up around me, startling me. I keep my expression impassive but wonder about their reaction. Am I doing enough? It doesn't feel like it, but their reaction is so strong, I can't help wondering if it means more than I think.

The man bows to me, and the others follow suit. I tell them to rise. Having their respect does nothing for me when I shouldn't need to make these changes in the first place.

I continue through the crowd, waving at people as I go by. They are eager, cheering and clapping, bright smiles on their faces and in their eyes. This time, there's no group holding back. The entire town seems to be here, cheering for what I've done. It's hard to fathom.

When I reach my carriage, Nash stands to one side, Inyi to another. My guards surround me, but the crowd is still within view. I turn toward them with my back to the carriage door. I raise a hand to silence them, and they all quiet down.

"My people, today is a day for celebration. We are returning what is rightfully yours and voiding the city tax." A great roar of approval fills the air. I give them several moments to express their joy before raising my hand again. "Given that your old ruler is no longer over the city, my lady-in-waiting, Inyi, is going to stay and oversee the voting in of a new ruler." She will make certain the city will find their way to a new leader.

"I know this is not how it's normally done," I continue. "Typically, I would choose someone as a replacement, but you know your needs better than I do. I want you to pick a fair and just leader. Whoever you select will be under my watch still, to put an end to the tyranny that should not exist in our country. But the choice is yours."

The crowd grows wilder than ever, screaming for joy and clapping. All sorts of noise resounds together to create a sound of joy. Someone from the crowd calls out, "All hail Queen Ryn."

Some pick up the saying. "Queen Ryn."

The man says in a second time. "All hail Queen Ryn."

More people pick it up. "Queen Ryn."

"All hail Queen Ryn," he says a third time.

"*Queen Ryn.*" The crowd screams my name.

I give them a wave and get in the carriage. It's difficult to know what to think. What to feel. This is so different than anything I've ever experienced. I'm grateful they're happy and hopeful that under Inyi's guidance they will pick a fair ruler, but this chanting my name, praising me… it's more than I know what to do with.

I do know one thing—it feels good to get something done.

The First Queen's presence is near. I can feel her in my mind. I wish I could read her. Know what she's thinking. Till now, she's only come to me like this when I'm in danger. Why would she choose now to draw near?

I don't know.

CHAPTER 26

THE NEXT STOP is blessedly uneventful. We are up the mountainside a little ways where the houses are on stilts on one side to accommodate the steep slope. Stairs go up the mountainside every ten or so houses, like a mini roadway. I spend part of the night going up and down those stairs for exercise, much to Jaku's dismay. He keeps me surrounded with guards, which means they are huffing and puffing right along with me.

The night air is crisp against my skin, kissing it with its coolness. When I spoke to the First Queen last night and asked her why she came to me, she said that she always wants to be with me to help and it's finally getting easier to do so. After a night speaking with her, I wake for a breakfast banquet with a group who are mildly receptive. Though they aren't as warm as I hoped for, they are generous with their things, giving me gifts of cloth, homemade pots, and beads.

When I ask Nash about it, he shrugs. Surprisingly, Inkga has an explanation. "They are a deeply caring people, but they don't show it outwardly. It is a sign of disgrace to show too much feeling, but the giving of gifts is a sign that they respect you."

"How do you know this?"

"I've been here once, with Queen Deedra." She pauses before adding, "She didn't receive as many gifts as you. She was cold to the country, and they were cold right back. It was in the later part of her ruling, years after she raised the taxes. They didn't appreciate it."

Neither would I.

After another day at the village, where the people show me songs and dance, we head to our last city. The ride isn't long—just half a day—and we reach Wolta. The city is full of people with big, eager eyes. Eager to see me, or eager to get rid of me?

My party is directed to the main building, where we are served dinner. For once, Nash is sitting by me. Seems like our hosts have kept him away from me ever since we left Indell. But not tonight.

I try not to pay much attention to him, but it's only right that I converse with my dinner partner. Though Mother is on my other side and likes to talk a lot, I'm aware of Nash next to me and the buzz of excitement tingling through my right side, where he's sitting.

It would be all too easy to lean over and brush against him. To take his hand under the table. To press a kiss on his forehead—no, his lips.

"Are you listening, darling?" Mother's voice cuts through my daydreaming.

"I have a lot on my mind." And none of it what it's supposed to be. "What were you saying?"

"I asked if you're going to attend the celebration tonight, or if you're going to bed. You look tired."

Not as tired as Nash. The dark circles under his eyes have grown worse. "I'll attend, but anyone else should only do so if they desire."

"I'd be happy to accompany you." She continues chatting away, though this time turning her attention to Father, who's sitting on her other side.

She continues chatting away, though this time turning her attention to Carver who's sitting on her other side.

This city has been welcoming so far, but I want to know more about it. There are so many of them, I wish I had a better way to communicate with them. If Inyi was here, she might have some ideas.

Dinner finishes before I know it, without time to enjoy anything. Boplou, the leader of this city, heads toward me, a grin gracing her face. She curtsies when she gets to me, and I motion for her to rise.

"Your Majesty, we are so happy to have you in our city that we would like to present you with a gift."

I lift an eyebrow. What could they be giving me? And why? There's always a purpose behind everything. I can't imagine her doing this out of the goodness of her heart. Is there something hiding behind the gesture?

She turns and points toward a nearby dark hallway. There's a glimmer of movement toward its lower half. A glow of golden eyes, not entirely human, shines dimly. A moment later, a sleek, black-furred animal that would reach my waist saunters in front of a woman.

The animal has thick, long fangs and the build of a cat. A really, really large cat. It has two tails that sway along with the woman walking beside it. She is something of a mystery herself. She's bald, her blue eyes standing out against skin so pale it almost shimmers. She's lithe but strong, with muscles in her arms. Her white pants and shirt are almost the same color as she is, without the shimmer.

I'm not sure which of them poses the greater danger.

Those gathered in the room ooh and aah over them. Little bits of chatter reach me but not clear enough to make out. The excitement I can hear, though. We've never seen anything like this before.

Boplou lifts one side of her mouth. "This is Venda. The fila is Puneah."

"Fila?" I eye the creature with a new appreciation. "I thought they were only myth."

"To most, they are." Venda's voice is melodic. "In Faner, we have a few, though their species has almost died out."

Venda stops several feet from me, but the fila continues to approach. The sleek animal stalks forward—a huge, threatening cat. Usually, I'm only afraid of Daros, but this fila has my knees shaking almost as bad as when he was around.

Puneah stops inches from me. Its hot breath tickles my hand as it smells me.

"She's getting to know you," Venda says.

I almost ask if she bites, but it's a useless question. With those fangs, of course she does.

Puneah's tails twitch as she moves to my other hand. Her wet nose pushes right up against my hand, touching my wooden ring. Her tails suddenly stick straight out before one wraps itself around the other.

"What does that mean?" My voice doesn't betray my fear. Good.

Venda cocks her head. "We will speak later about your new pet."

"Wait. This fila is mine?"

Puneah nudges my hand playfully. Or maybe hungrily. It's difficult to tell.

"She is a gift to you from the country of Faner. Your ruler of Wolta personally contacted us and asked us for such a gift," Venda says.

Boplou is beaming.

What am I going to do with a pet? And is it a pet, or a way to kill me without raising a hand? "Thank you both for your generosity."

Puneah continues butting up against my hand, tail still twisted up.

"If it pleases you," Venda says, "I will accompany you back to Indell and teach you and your servants how to care for a fila."

Another person I have to watch my back with. I put a smile on, anyway. "That would be wonderful."

"Puneah, come." Venda pats her leg.

The fila stops moving my hand and goes to her, tails uncurling. I don't let the tension ease from my shoulders.

"We will await you in your rooms," Venda says.

Now I won't want to go to sleep from worry over them. "Very well."

Boplou takes a step closer as woman and fila disappear into the hall. "That's the first fila I've ever seen. It was magnificent," she says.

Were we looking at the same creature? Then again, despite the dangerous gleam in Puneah's eyes, it was an interesting creature. Myths say that they have something to do with magic.

I wonder what Puneah would make of the Mortum Tura. Not that she could tell me. "It sure was something. Thank you again for the gift."

She blushes. "It was nothing."

I think back on my earlier thoughts. "If you don't mind my asking, what do the people of your city think of me as a ruler?"

Boplou pulls the chain around her neck out from under her dress and brushes her fingers across a pendant. The way she moves her fingers in small circles makes me think she's unaware she's doing it. She says, "The truth is the people are uncertain about you. They don't know what to think, and we hear such differing reports."

"Why give me such a grand gift, then?" One she must have been planning since I drank the Mortum Tura to make it happen.

She looks down at her necklace and drops it. "Let's just say I had a good feeling about you."

That's all? A good feeling? "You trust that?"

She grins. "I do. I know you'll make a fine leader."

She has more confidence in me than I do. Maybe I can do something to earn it. "Is there something you need from me, for your people or city?"

"There is one thing."

When she doesn't continue, I ask, "What is it?"

She glances around the room. "The dam near our city is getting old and falling apart. I'm afraid it will collapse and all the homes below it will be caught in a flood if some work isn't done on it soon. We've been trying to fix it, but have only come up with temporary solutions."

"Why not fix it permanently?"

"We don't have enough money."

"That's easy. I'll release some from the crown. I've been looking for projects like this to make the country better while creating jobs. Plus, I want to help out before the dam breaks."

"You would do that?" Her eyes sparkle with tears. Of hope?

"Of course. Why are you so surprised?"

She looks at the floor, grabbing her necklace once again. "I shouldn't be. Not with you. It's just that Queen Deedra never came to visit us. We're too close to the border of Faner, and things aren't as fancy out here. When I sent her notes of what we needed, they went unanswered."

I feel an urge to take her hand, to let her know how serious I am, but I refrain. "Look at me." Once she does so, I say, "I am not Queen Deedra, nor will I ever be. I promise to help you and the city. My people deserve that." And so much more.

"Thank you, Your Majesty. Thank you."

"You're most welcome. If you'll excuse me, I need to speak with my Head Advisor so I can get this in the works as soon as possible."

"Certainly. Sleep well, Your Majesty."

She curtsies, then flitters over to another group. I don't have to go to Nash; he comes to me. Together, we walk toward my rooms, though I'm all too aware of the guards around us.

I quickly explain the situation with the dam. "Do you think we can handle this?"

"I'll get on it as soon as we're finished talking here."

"Thank you. Let me know what you need, and I'll see that you have it."

He nods. "I will."

"Did you spot what Faner and Boplou gifted me?" I ask him.

"I did. I never thought I'd live to see a fila."

"You and me both. I thought they were legend."

I lower my voice, though I'm certain the guards can still hear us. "How are you?"

"Excited to see a fila up close."

I laugh. "You're crazy for wanting to get close to that thing."

"You did."

Not by choice. "Didn't you see its teeth?"

"Yes, and still, it treated you well."

"No guarantee it's going to stay that way," I mutter.

He gives me a smile so big it nearly melts me on the spot. "Have I finally found something you're afraid of?"

I scoff. "Of course not."

"Then you won't mind letting it smell you again?"

"I'm certain it will." Unfortunately.

He chuckles. It's oh-so-good to hear the sound. Maybe he's recovering some. Finding himself again.

We reach my room, and Nash opens the door for Jaku to scout out the room. Once he's assured of its safety, he ushers Julina in, then Nash, and finally me. The rest of my guards stay outside my room, positioned either at the window or in front of my door.

This building is smaller than Fulla's but still with enough room to house me like others think I need. I'd be happy with a small corner somewhere, but apparently that's not fitting my station.

Venda bows a welcome. "Puneah has been anxious to see you again."

I eye the fila. "How do you know?"

"You will learn." She turns her attention to the animal. "Puneah is special among the filas. My Queen personally helped pick her out for you."

Wonderful. Now I have to worry another ruler is trying to kill me, this time by pet.

Venda continues. "She thought, given your profession before being a queen, that you would prefer a black animal instead of a white one. The better to hide her with you when you go on excursions."

What does that mean? Does the queen of Faner expect me to still be an assassin? Maybe I'm overthinking what she said. Maybe she wants to be on my good side so I won't come after her. Not that we have much relations with other countries. I'll have to ask my Head of Foreign Relations what she knows about Faner. "That was thoughtful."

She eyes those with me. "I would like to speak with you privately, if that's all right."

I glance at Julina and Nash. Is there anything Venda could say that I don't want the two of them to hear? Doubtful. "You can speak freely. Both of them will keep whatever you share confidential."

"Are you certain?"

"I am. I trust these two with my life."

"Very well, then." Venda crouches down on Puneah's level, whispers something, and when she stands, Puneah comes to me and nudges my hand again, tails twisting together. "This is what I wished to speak to you of. The twisting tails."

"What do they mean?"

"Any guesses?"

"The only thing difference between my two hands is this one has a ring on it."

"What do you know of this ring?"

"Not much. I found it in the treasury." And was drawn to it. Liked it. Wanted to wear it. Nothing that should be attracting such attention.

"Filas' tails twist together when they detect magic. The stronger the magic, the tighter their tails are twisted together."

Magic? "Are you suggesting there's something different about my ring?"

"Not just *something*. Magic. I know your country doesn't deal in magic much, but that doesn't mean it's extinct."

I rise my hand away from Puneah, and her tail untwists. I brush my fingers across the ring. "What does it do?"

"That I cannot tell you."

That's helpful. "Does this work with any magical item?"

"It does."

"How do I get Puneah to stop paying attention to the object?"

"Once you acknowledge the item, she will stop. Put your arm back down and you will see."

I do as she says. Puneah gives my hand a once over before making a circle around me. Her tail remains untwisted. "How does she know I acknowledged what she was trying to tell me?"

"How does such a creature know to show you magical items to begin with? It's a mystery, as much as why our moons are different colors."

I nod. Makes sense. Sort of. "How do I find out what the ring does?"

"Experimenting."

"Do you have any ideas what it might do?" Nash asks. "Examples you could give us?"

Venda laces her fingers together and rests them on her stomach. "There are many things magic can do. It is harder, I think, for you in Valcora to think of such things since you are not accustomed to thoughts that turn towards magic. If there is an idea, it can be done with magic, under the right circumstances."

Her answer leaves me more confused than ever. "Like the Mortum Tura?"

Her eyes grow dark. "That drink is a type of magic. Yes."

"Do you not like it?" I ask.

Her gaze drops. "It is not a question of whether I like it or not. In Faner, our Queen is chosen by the gods, not magic."

In a country where magic is more prevalent, I would expect their ruler to be picked through a similar means as ours. Back to the question at hand. "You have no way to tell what magic my ring does?"

"No."

"And no examples?"

"They are as far reaching as your imagination. If you can think it, it can be done, given the time and ingredients. Knowledge is a key factor as well. You could spell a pebble to give you confidence. A tunic to give you luck. Perhaps a chair to bring comfort to the user. Magic is as varying as the people using it."

"Is there a way to tell if it's bad?"

Puneah curls up at my feet, appearing less fearsome except for her fangs.

"Not unless you are trained," Venda says.

"Can you tell if this ring is bad?" Nash asks.

Venda takes a step closer. "If Your Majesty will permit me, I may be able to tell by holding it."

Since the ring doesn't seem to do anything anyway, and I want to know if it's evil, I take it off and drop it into her outstretched hand.

She doesn't put it on, but brings it closer to her face, twirling it slowly as she looks at it. After a moment, she clasps her hands around it and closes her eyes. I exchange a glance first with Nash, then with Julina. Neither seem more sure of what to do than I am.

She remains silent for a while. I ask, "Are you detecting anything?"

Her eyes dart open with their vividness. "It is hard to read, and

I'm not skilled at such things, but I would say whatever it has, it is a good sort of magic. Of course I can't guarantee such things, but I'm fairly confident."

Fairly. So comforting.

I hold out my hand, and she drops the ring back on my palm. I put it on but hardly realize a difference. I want to know what it does. It's the most interest I've had in magic since the Mortum Tura. Would the First Queen know anything about this?

"What can you tell us about this fila?" Julina asks, probably worried about my safety.

As Venda talks of how Puneah is much friendlier than she looks to people she likes, but is mean to those she doesn't trust, and all sorts of other traits I don't care about, I think about the ring on my finger.

It's light, barely noticeable. Almost nothing.

But what magic does it contain? Is it helping me with something? Hurting me? Or something so mundane I don't even notice? The latter most like. Not that it will ever matter. I just like the ring.

CHAPTER 27

THE FIRST QUEEN STANDS, arms folded, as she stares into the distant colors. Does she ever get bored here? Long for more?

"Yes."

Being bored here and wanting more must be hard. "Is there any way you can do more than this life?"

She glances at me, her gaze somber. "This is enough for me."

I'm about to ask more, but she says, "What did you think of the gift from Boplou and Faner?"

"You already know."

She settles into a nonexistent seat. "It's fine to be scared of things."

"I'm not scared. I don't see the purpose of having a pet. It's not something I ever needed before. Nothing's changed about that."

"It's up to you, but you may find the animal useful."

The fila is mystical, but not for me. "Did Queen Deedra ever meet Boplou?"

She shakes her head.

"What about Faner? Do you know anything about that country and its people?" *I need information. She's been around longer than anyone else; she must know something about them.*

"The truth is I know little. I came to this country with a group from far away. *We found this valley protected. It was what we were looking for, but there were no other countries around Valcora when we came here."*

I wrinkle my eyebrows. "How long ago was that?" *How long has she been in this state?*

"A millennia, more or less."

That has to be an exaggeration. It's so long; I can't fathom it.

"It has been a long time in some ways, but short in many others. It is true, though."

No wonder there were so many portraits in the hallway. Even then, I can't be sure they're all there. It may have been a tradition they started some time after the Mortum Tura was developed.

"Well after."

"How many queens came before that?"

"Too many to count. But none of this is information that will help you. What you need to focus on are things that will help you be a good queen now."

I'm about to contradict her but stop myself. I may think it's good to learn from our history, but that doesn't mean she has to agree. "When did we start getting information about other countries?"

"Several hundred years after we settled here. We made a deal that they would stay out of our valley at first, but it turned out to be mostly unneeded since it's so difficult to get people in and out. Every few hundred years, we make contact with someone from the outside, like you did today."

"That long? You'd think people would be more curious than that."

"That's only official. There are probably many who have gone from our country to another and vice versa that I don't know about. Nothing to make a splash over."

So people do travel back and forth between the two countries. Interesting.

"Yes, but again, this doesn't help you become a better queen. We need to find out how long this Venda will be helping around with the fila.

While I'd like to learn what we can about the creature, I'd like to see her off before too long."

I shrug. "She seems all right, but I will keep a close eye on her."

"It would give me peace of mind."

I stifle my thoughts. I shouldn't be like that to her. "Sorry. I don't mean to be so ornery today."

"You've been busy these last few weeks. No one could blame you for being a little cross." She gives a gentle smile. "You're going to wake up soon. I can feel myself fading. Is there anything else you'd like to discuss?"

"What do you know about this wooden ring? Venda said it was magic —that Puneah detected it—but I don't know what it does."

She purses her lips. "I'm not sure. I recognize most pieces out of the treasury, but this is one of the few that came about when I wasn't present."

I glance down at the ring that followed me to this world. "It is a plain piece of jewelry." But there's something about it that I like.

"So keep it." She waves away the rest of my thoughts. "We'll talk more later."

"I'll be here."

"And so will I."

* * *

THE LAST DAY before we head back to the palace—to home—is bittersweet. I've enjoyed my time among my fellow countrymen, but I'm anxious to get back to things. Surprisingly, I miss the usual work.

And I miss time alone with Nash.

I should no longer be alone with him, though, just like has been done on the tour.

There's loud cheering from outside the closed doors. It's time to get going and face the crowd.

"The people are anxious to spend time with you before they see you off," Boplou says.

"I feel the same about them." There's to be a celebration. My party is here, except for about half my guards, who are preparing my way outside. Some of the guards from Wolta are stationed nearby to help offset the difference.

Mother and Father are in the back, where Nash was speaking with them, but he's making his way forward now. I avert my gaze. "It sounds as if it's going to be exciting."

"I'm glad you think so. It should be quite the showing."

"Your people aren't upset with me, for changing taxes so much?" I dare ask.

She pauses. "Some are, but I wouldn't worry about them. They will learn how to deal with their feelings sooner or later. Especially when they find out you are helping to fix the dam."

"It was the least I could do. The people pay their taxes; it's only fair that the money goes into things they need."

The massive door in front of us opens, the roaring of the crowd growing louder. Suddenly I wish I was back in my room with Puneah and Venda. They are less intimidating than the mass I'm to go through.

Nash gives me a smile as he reaches my side. I work to keep the butterflies in my stomach from showing on my face.

A man comes forward and bows. "Your Majesty, they are ready for you."

"Very well."

I step forward, the group moving with me. We head out the door and down the steps, and the hoard cheers wildly at the sight of me. I wave and smile, accustomed to the setup the guards have: a line of them on each side of the walkway protecting me from the people.

Or maybe the people from me.

I continue to wave and smile, feeling awkward, though I'm

getting a little more accustomed to it since I've been doing this more regularly.

It grows quieter but still loud. The crowd is more subdued, their eyes heavy with sleep, like they've been up working all night. And still, they cheer, joining their hands and raising them in the air as a sign of enthusiasm. Some people clap. Call my name. "Queen Ryn. Queen Ryn." It's a little disconcerting. What am I supposed to do?

I toss the thought aside. I shouldn't have too much more to go, and then I'll be finished with this parade. I think. It's hard to know for certain. It feels as if I've been doing this for a while.

Something is different, though I can't figure what. None of my party is by me, but that's not so unusual. The crowd isn't cheering like they were before, but a person can only cheer for so long. No, it's something else. Something wrong.

It hits me.

None of my guards are around me.

These are all guards from Wolta.

It shouldn't worry me, but my gut tightens. This isn't right.

I put a hand on my dagger, but it's too late. A hard object smashes into me from behind, knocking me to my knees. A black flash comes my way as someone moves to kick me. I roll away and end up on my back with a group of angry guards looking down at me. They pull out their swords as I take out my daggers.

This is not a good position to be in.

Where are my guards?

There's no more time to think.

I'm fending off blades, trying to kick at the greatest amount of them as I can. There are too many. I've never faced so many opponents at one time before. I don't know how I'll survive this.

I stab my dagger into the closest leg, and a man lets out a howl. But it's not enough. A sword is coming down toward me, and I don't have enough time to block it.

Out of nowhere, a second sword clashes into the first, and

Nash is here, standing over me, with his back to me. While everyone is distracted by him, I get to my feet and move so our backs almost touch.

"Where are the other guards?" I yell.

The attacker across from me smirks and comes at me. I whip my blades around so fast there's nothing but a blur of motion before he's on the ground.

"They're being held back by more attackers," Nash hollers back.

That's all the chance we have to talk. Swords are flying at me in a rush. I let loose my throwing dagger and reach for another one even as I block a blade. There's a yelp as my throw makes contact with someone, but I don't stop to survey the damage. Too much metal is coming at me too fast.

I move on instinct, letting my arms do the job I've been trained for my whole life. My feet don't keep still as the uneven cobblestone beneath them tries to trip me. I push myself.

A sword slices into my arm from the right. I kick at my attacker, aiming for where it will hurt the most. He falls to the ground. Blood drips down my arm, but the metallic smell filling the air isn't just from me, but also from the men I've hit.

There are still too many of them. We need help. No. We need a miracle.

I pretend there's all the help in the world. That my arm isn't injured. That this is a test Daros sent. If I pass, I'll be rewarded. If I fail, I'll be sent to *the* room. Never mind that he doesn't live in that house anymore. It's a good motivation.

I attack harder and faster than before, pushing myself beyond my limits as I gasp for air. My blades ward off attack after attack, but I'm weakening.

Finally, the assault stops. I stand, chest heaving, blades up. Several men and women are on the ground around me, but more await. The crowd is screaming and running, but one of the guards has a woman held against him, his blade to her stomach.

"Stop fighting now, or we'll kill the woman," the man yells.

I don't think; I react. The dagger is flying toward him before I know what's happening. It lands in the arm holding the blade to the woman, forcing him to drop it with a cry. The woman takes off, but not away from the fight. Toward me.

She stands in front of me, turns her back to me, and shouts, "Leave her alone."

"Don't. You'll get yourself killed." The words are out of my mouth before I can stop them.

She doesn't move.

The people that were screaming and scattering take notice of her and stop their fleeing. I move to shove the woman behind me, without touching her.

"Ah, ah, ah," the man says. "You can't protect her. You can't even protect yourself."

I've had it with this guy. I let another dagger fly straight at his belly. I don't watch the aftereffect, except to see his grimace. "Anyone else want to mess with me?"

The remaining guards shift their weight. I must have taken out their leader. They don't seem to know what to do. Then, with a burst of energy, they come at me.

Julina joins the fray, followed by several guards. They must have fought their way to me. They aren't as sharp as usual, but with them comes relief, despite their being tired.

It only takes a few moments to finish off the crew of turned guards who won't hand themselves over.

"Are you all right, Your Majesty?" Julina asks.

"I'm fine. Just a minor cut. Take these rogues to Boplou's home, and I'll interview them when I'm done here."

She nods.

"You should get that cut looked at first," Nash says.

I whirl around to take him in. There's not a scratch on him, though he's breathing hard. "Thank you for coming to my aid," I say.

"Always." The look in his eyes is so intense, I have to turn away before I do something stupid like kiss him.

I turn my attention toward the girl who almost got herself killed and probably saved my life. "What is your name?"

"Edin."

"Edin, thank you for saving my life. You have the crown's highest respect."

Her eyes widen. "I was doing what anyone would."

I motion to the crowd now gathered around us. "Not anyone. As a tribute to your bravery, I'm awarding you twenty gold pieces."

A gasp sounds throughout the crowd.

"Thank you, Your Majesty." She gushes and curtsies. "I will always remember your goodness and generosity."

Interesting reaction from someone who watched me injure several people.

A single person begins to clap, followed by another, and another. Soon, the remaining crowd is clapping and cheering, more loudly than ever before.

Somehow, it feels like I've won their love and loyalty.

CHAPTER 28

NASH WALKS at my side toward Boplou's home, silent.

I ignore the murmur of voices around us. I want to know what he's thinking—what troubles are plaguing him, or if it's something else entirely keeping him silent.

When we reach the building, I'm ushered inside and to the nearest room, where a healer is waiting for me. My party waits outside while he wraps up my arm.

It hurts more now that adrenaline isn't pumping through me but not bad enough to show. I've had much, much worse.

When the healer is done with me, I insist he look at Nash and the rest of my guards. Nash, Jaku, and Julina refuse, instead following me to Boplou, who is waiting across the hall. Servants come and go from her like a hive of bees. As soon as she sees me, she puts up a hand to stop them.

Boplou is pale. "Are you all right?"

"Fine." Not at all what I'm worried about right now. "Why weren't the guards better vetted?"

"I already had the first of them interrogated. We should discuss what's happened."

I narrow my lips. "Very well."

"Come with me, Your Highness, and I will explain what I know." She motions to a room behind her.

This had better be good.

Julina enters the room before me and gives me the all-clear sign. I go in, Nash and Jaku right behind me, my temperature increasing with each step.

Boplou stands in the middle of the windowless room. It has several chairs placed in a circle, except in front of a low fireplace. No wonder it's warm in here. "Please, be seated," she says.

My body is rather exhausted. I don't hesitate before taking a seat, and the others do as well, except Julina and Jaku.

"Those were your guards who attacked me," I say. "What happened?" And I hope she wasn't involved in this. I like her too much for that.

"It would seem they had an outside influence that corrupted them. I greatly apologize, Your Majesty. If I knew any of this was going on, I never would have relied on them to help guard you."

"How do we know you aren't in cahoots with them?"

"I'm afraid my word will have to suffice for now, though you can have your people check the facts after I relate the tale to you."

"Very well. Go on."

"It would seem some of my guards have been getting direction from an outside source. I don't know who yet, though I'm trying to find out."

Daros comes to mind, but I'm not so sure. Why would he be affecting a town all the way out in Wolta? And wouldn't he want to kill me himself? The situation doesn't make sense. But then who else would it be? I brush him away to focus on the task at hand. "Keep going."

"Whoever it is, they don't like how you've bounced around the taxes. They've convinced my guards that, in doing so, you've weakened yourself in front of the people. They believe getting rid of you is the best hope for our country. Then a new queen will be chosen, and hopefully bring them stability."

Does it always have to come down to those stupid taxes?

Nash shifts at my side, probably uncomfortable at the reminder of what I tried to do to save his life. I ignore him for now. As much as I want to, there's nothing I can say in front of witnesses to make him feel better. "Where have you put my would-be assassins?" I ask.

"Those who aren't hurt or have been tended to are in my dungeon. Otherwise, they're waiting to be seen by a healer, under guard from those I still trust."

"Very well. Thank you for this information. Julina, will you please escort Boplou out while I discuss this with my Head Advisor? Keep an eye on her for me. No offense, Boplou. I want to trust you, but until I figure out all the facts, I need to be careful."

"No offense taken." Boplou stands. "Please let me know if you have any other questions or think of a way I can help you."

"I will."

She leaves the room, and I wave Julina and Jaku out and close the door behind them.

I don't wait. I throw myself in Nash's arms, heedless of my injury. He wraps his arms around me, making soothing sounds.

"It's going to be all right," he says.

I pull myself out of his arms but don't let go of his hand. "How do you know that? It seems like everywhere I go someone has a problem with me and is trying to kill me in order for the Mortum Tura to select a new queen. This country is full of mad people."

"Right now, I have to agree with you." His voice is calm. Reassuring.

"I've missed you," I say.

He brushes a hand across my cheek. "I've missed you too."

I sigh. There are so many things I want to ask him. I settle for, "What are we going to do about this?"

"I'll check around and see if I can find any connection between Boplou and the attackers, but I'm inclined to believe she's telling the truth."

"So am I. Why else would she go to the trouble of gifting me a fila? Plus, she's been so nice. Kindness can be faked, but my gut trusts her."

"That's a fairly good indication, but I'll still check her out."

"And what do we do if she's guilty?"

"We'll deal with that if it arises."

That's all we need to discuss. I should excuse him. Let him go to work. Instead, I give his hand a squeeze, enjoying the feel of it within my own. "How are you doing?"

"Surviving, now that I'm with you."

Sweet, but not good enough if it means he's still struggling other times. "Have you been getting any sleep?"

He lets go of my hand. "I sleep enough."

"The dark circles under your eyes say otherwise."

He stands. "I'm going to check around."

That's what I get for opening my mouth. "If you insist. I care about you is all. That's why I say the things I do."

He nods but doesn't look at me.

As he goes out the door, I wonder if we'll ever connect like we might have before he was taken. Not that it matters. Even if we do, we'll never be together.

CHAPTER 29

THE CARRIAGE COMES to a rolling stop, surprising me. We weren't supposed to stop again until tonight, but it's midday. Nash comes to the open window, putting away a small knife and wooden token he had been carving in his pocket. "We're going to have an extra place to visit. I wanted to let you know. The owner of one of the mines we were looking at purchasing got a hold of us and said he is interested in a meeting."

Butterflies flitter around my stomach. "Thanks for letting me know."

We take off again, and I wonder why my nerves are getting the better of me. Perhaps it's because I want this to work out.

"This is good news," Inkga says. "Isn't it?"

"I hope so." If he will sell to us. I can't be sure they will. Then again, there's no reason for them not to.

It doesn't take long to reach our destination. When I step out of the carriage, the first sight that greets me is a surly-looking man in his fifties, dressed in fine things.

"I didn't realize the person looking to purchase my land was the queen," he says in a hard voice.

No bowing. No *Your Majesty*. This man clearly doesn't like me.

Why? "You didn't know it was the government wanting your mine?"

"No."

He turns and heads to the nearby mansion. It's an elegant house, fitting someone who's made a lot of money, but having money isn't what I'm worried about. It's whether or not I can purchase the mine for the government from him.

I hurry to catch up to him, my entourage surrounding me. "I would like to discuss purchasing the mine."

"No."

He increases his pace until we're almost to the door.

"Can you at least explain to me why you're no longer interested?" I ask.

"No."

Chatty fellow. "Please give me one reason you're not willing to sell."

He whips around. "I'm willing to sell. Just not to a group who doesn't take care of their own people. Not to someone who can't see the needy right in front of them."

I open my mouth to respond, but he's at the door. It opens before he touches it, and a woman about his age stands inside. She's plump, with long, dark hair mixed with graying strands and eyes that are far too familiar.

The woman who taught me to read.

"You." Venom laces my word. The woman who taught me to read. She's the one who was going to take me away from Daros but never came back for me. I have a wild urge to smack her across the face. To hurt her like she hurt me. "You left me in the hands of a madman when you said you'd save me."

Her face goes pale. "It can't be."

"What can't be?" Irritation clings to me.

"It's you." She cries and steps outside, holding out her hands like she's going to touch me.

Before she can get to me, the man reaches out and gently

guides her away. When he speaks, the gruffness is gone from his voice. "This is the queen. If you touch her, you'll be killed."

Her eyes go wide. "The queen? How did you become queen? You were under the influence of that *man*."

I cross my arms. "Didn't you hear the rumors? The Shadow Wraith became queen. Daros outed me. I sent him to prison, and he escaped."

"You are the Shadow Wraith? Did Daros put you up to becoming queen?" Her face is still pale, though color is coming back to it.

"No. I ran away, like you were supposed to help me do years ago. I did it myself. I wanted to die after the life he put me through. The life you were supposed to save me from, but you never returned."

"This is the girl?" the man asks the woman.

She nods, now more green than pale.

I hold my arms tighter against me as if that will keep the hurt in. Though I fear I know what they're talking about, I ask, "What girl?"

"I wanted to save you." The woman's voice is shaky. "I tried. I came back for you, ready to run with all the supplies I could gather, but he was waiting for me. Had me beaten within an inch of my life, dropped me off in a far away village, and told me if I was ever to return, he'd torture you in front of me and then kill me in front of you. I wanted to save you, but I believed him and didn't know how to rescue you from such circumstances. I didn't want you to have to be tortured and witness my death."

I'm feeling a little green myself. "No. You ran off without me. You left me with him after giving me hope."

"Darling girl, I would have done anything for you."

"She tried to go back for you," the man says, looking much kinder now that his features have softened. "I stopped her. Said it was too dangerous."

I shake my head. "It can't be."

"I'm afraid it's true." The man pulls her closer as tears stream down her face.

She says, "I never forgave myself for not getting you out. I'm so sorry I failed you."

"I need to sit down."

She hurries to the doorway. "Forgive me. Please come in."

I head forward, but Jaku whispers, "Do you trust her?"

"It's difficult to say. At one point I did, and then I didn't. Now I'm uncertain."

He nods and motions for several guards to go in the house after the couple before allowing me to follow. The foyer we enter is a blur as we pass through it until we reach a sitting room. I collapse into the nearest chair.

The woman picks the chair closest to mine while her husband stands behind her and the rest of my party spreads out around the room.

"I'm so sorry," the woman says again. "I didn't want to leave you to that fate."

"You mean it? You didn't want to leave me there?"

Her expression somehow grows even more serious. "I promise you I would never have left you if I had any choice."

I swallow and grip the arms of the chair with my hands. Can I believe this? It falls in line with how she treated me before she disappeared. The story also fits Daros's personality, but I always thought she ran away without me. Or perhaps that she went home and forgot about me. That she didn't want me. Didn't love me the way she said she did. That she was one more person in a sea of many who didn't care. "I never even knew your name," I say.

"Kapeni. My name is Kapeni, and I've always wondered what happened to you. What your name was. You only ever told me it was *girl*."

I wince. "That's what he called me. The only thing I was ever called until I picked a name for myself. You may call me *Ryn*."

Tears course down her cheeks. "Ryn, I can't tell you how much it means to see you again. How happy I am to see you are well and thriving."

I don't know about thriving, but I'm doing better than I was when I was in Daros's hands.

"And you are the queen. I never thought my cherished one would become queen."

"I never expected it either." My words are faint.

"You said Daros was on the loose. Is he... after you?"

My voice is stronger. This is something I can answer. Something I know how to deal with. "He is, but I have a lot of protection now. He won't be getting to me if he's still around." My voice is stronger.

Her shoulders slump with relief. "Thank all of Valcora. I'm beyond thrilled you are safe from him."

As am I.

"I'm so glad you stumbled our way," she says.

"I'm not sure we stumbled as much as this man requested for us to come."

"I am Coplo," the man says. "And about the mine..."

The mine was the furthest thing from my mind. "What about it?"

"I may have been hasty, not wanting to sell it to you. Kapeni has always talked of your goodness, even in the home of that monster."

I glance at Mother and Father, who haven't spoken. If Kapeni knew Daros was evil, why didn't they? It doesn't matter. What's done is done.

"I may be willing to enter into negotiations with you," Coplo continues, "but I'll want some reassurance that it's not for greedy government fingers. That you are using it to help the people."

With Nash's help, I lay out the idea for buying the mine and using it to give citizens jobs while any profits will be invested into the country's infrastructure. The entire time, I keep glancing back at Kapeni. I can't believe I've found her.

"I like the sound of your plans," Coplo says. "I need safety measures to make certain it doesn't get abused in the future, but I believe we can come to an arrangement."

Kapeni beams. I can't help but grin. This is what I wanted, and when we arrived, I didn't think we'd be able to get it. "Thank you for your generosity. I'd be happy to add safety measures to the plans. Why don't you come to the capital when you're ready, and we can hash out the details? You can stay as guests at the palace."

"We would love that," Kapeni gushes. "We've always talked about going back to Indell, but never did."

I glance at Coplo. He says, "We would be delighted."

"That settles it, then," I say. "I look forward to seeing you at the palace as soon as is convenient for you."

We talk for several hours about her life and mine along with any little thought that comes to mind while the rest of my group except the guards are shown a place they can relax. Once we've talked a while, I introduce her to my parents, who don't seem to understand how much she means to me, but that's all right. As long as I know, that's what matters.

Kapeni invites us to stay the night, and with little hesitation, I accept. It's wonderful talking with her until late into the night. She's everything I remember and so much more. The next morning, when it's time to leave, the couple sees us out.

"I wish I could give you a hug," I whisper to Kapeni.

"I do as well, cherished one. But we will stay in contact. I promise you that. I won't disappear from your life again."

I grin. "I'll hold you to it."

CHAPTER 30

AFTER THE LONG JOURNEY HOME, I have the strangest urge to jump on my bed. Instead, I assist Inkga in putting away clothes from the trunks.

"You don't have to help," she says. "I can manage."

"It's still weird to have everyone do everything for me all the time."

"I can't imagine what it would be like, to go from doing everything myself to having someone wanting to do everything for me. Don't worry—I don't actually mind the help. Just know you don't have to do it, if you don't want to."

As we put things away, I say, "I'm so excited we met Kapeni."

"I can't believe she wanted to save you all this time, but Daros scared her off."

This was one of the things we talked about on the way back, but I keep bringing it up because I'm so thrilled to find another person from my childhood that actually cared. "I can't, either. Yet another reason to not trust Daros, if I needed one."

"That man deserves to be executed."

I pause midair before putting a shirt in the closet. "You think so?"

"Don't you?"

Slowly, I put the shirt away. "I do. It's just I promised not to kill again. I've already killed so much, I don't want to do it again."

"You don't have to do it."

"It would still be under my orders." More blood on my hands.

"Maybe, but how many will die if he isn't executed?"

Something to ponder.

We continue to chat as we work when there's a knock on my sitting room door.

"I'll answer it," Inkga says.

A moment later, she comes back with a stack of letters. "These all arrived for you while we were gone. Why don't you go through them while I finish up here?"

I'd rather help her than do paperwork, but it has to be done. "All right."

I sit in the middle of the bed, making piles as I read through them. Most are thanks for visiting a ruler's town. Some are notes from people, thanking me for other things that should be standard. A few are complaints. I get to one down toward the bottom, and my hands still.

It's speckled with blood

I grit my teeth.

Whatever it says, I can deal with it. I have to.

But please, *please* don't be another person I care about, being taken or hurt.

"Inkga, get Jaku." He'll want to see this.

She hurries from the room while I break the seal of the letter and read.

WE'RE RESUMING *control of the country. We won't stand for what you've done. The attempted poisoning was a warning, to show you how much power we have. The tax change Fulla made under the direction of Queen*

Deedra was because of our influence. The guards' attack was orchestrated by us.

Lower our taxes, or there will be more of this to come.

Last warning.

The Kurah

I SWALLOW past the thickening of my throat as I reread the letter. How dare they? My hands shake, but with rage not fear. Had they come to me in a more civil manner, we might have worked this out. But this? This is declaring war on me as a ruler. They'll throw my country into chaos.

I have to do something.

Jaku hurries in the room, Inkga behind him, brows furrowed into a frown that mars her features.

"What is it?" Jaku asks. "What happened?"

I hand him the note.

He reads it and swears. "Sorry about the language, Ryn."

"I'm more worried about the Kurah's control over the nation. Do you think they are as deeply involved as the note says they are?"

"I don't know, and I don't want to find out the hard way. We'll have guards on you like when we were touring the country, keeping someone with you at all times, even in your quarters."

"I don't think they're going to attack me. They did that and lost."

"But they could have others attack you. The guards almost overcame you in Wolta. If things hadn't changed in a hurry, you could have been killed, and they would have been free to find someone else to put on the throne."

"Who's causing problems this time? Daros?" Inkga asks.

I motion for Jaku to show her the note, and she pales as she reads it. I say, "You don't have to keep serving me. It puts you in harm's way. You should stay safe."

"I don't mind." But the quiver in her voice says she does.

"I'm serious, Inkga. I don't want anything to happen to you. To anyone." I've got to find a way to stop them. How can I when they are such a large group? I must find out who their leader is and stop them.

"I know, but I'll be fine. I'm just a servant."

"And I'm determined to keep you safe and free," Jaku says.

"As am I." The question now is: do we tell others about this, or leave it a secret? I'm inclined to keep it between us, but I don't know if that's the right answer. I ask the others what they think.

"Fear spreads fear," Inkga says. "If you tell others, it will make them worry more. We should keep it between us."

"I agree," Jaku says. "Other than letting your guards know you need extra protection, I don't think we need to share specifics."

"Very well."

"I'll assign more guards now," Jaku says, "unless you have something else you needed from me."

"That's all."

"I'll get Wilric in here right away." He leaves the room.

I turn to Inkga. "Could you set up a meeting with Mina for me? Also, I need to speak with Jem." I need to talk to my Head of Foreign Relations and answer some longer standing questions plus make decisions about what to do about them. Just because the Kurah are threatening me doesn't mean I can't continue my job as queen.

"Of course. As soon as I finish cleaning up." She hurries to her chores, but I think it has more to do with not wanting to leave me alone than it does with getting things done.

Wilric enters the room with a nod at me. It's going to be a long time dealing with people when I'd rather be alone.

What am I going to do about this? How can I calm the Kurah down without upsetting the rest of the nation?

CHAPTER 31

JEM TAKES a chair nearby in my sitting room while Wilric watches. The guards outside my window and door have increased in number, to the point where I'm not sure why he needs to be here, but for once, I don't feel like arguing.

"Thank you for coming," I tell Jem.

"Certainly. How were your countryside visits?"

"Valuable." If nothing else, I learned who some of my enemies are. Plus, I got a giant, lethal cat that could bite my head off any moment I'm around her. Luckily, the fila is with her handler, who is teaching people across the palace about her.

"I'm glad to hear it. I was hoping it would go well for you."

"How were things here?" I ask her.

"Like you'd expect. Things ran like normal. No problems to report, though I did have a hard time getting Timit to always cooperate."

Welcome to my world. "Anything serious?"

"Nothing I couldn't handle. He should have some reports coming for you."

"I saw them." Though it's harder to remember them when I got a note from the Kurah at the same time. "Did you?"

She nods. "I looked them over before I sent them."

"Your conclusions?"

She lifts an eyebrow. "Timit may not be entirely on your side, but he's coming around, I believe. His reports looked good for the projects you sent us while you were gone. He's already securing funds to help with what you requested. I think it's a wise move, for the country and for you."

"Thank you." It's high praise coming from her.

"Forgive me, but are you all right?"

"Why?" Am I doing something wrong?

"You don't seem quite yourself."

"I'm fine."

She nods, but her eyes say she doesn't believe me as she darts her gaze to where Wilric stands. Or maybe she just wants to look at him. He's studiously ignoring her, but the tension between them is so thick, I can almost feel it.

I ask, "Would you like to stay? I'm having Mina come talk about Faner."

"I'd like that. I heard you came home with a pet from there. Is it really a fila?" The last word holds a hint of awe.

I'd be more awed if I wasn't afraid it was going to bite my hand off. "It is."

"I'd like to see it."

"Send one of the servants for Venda and Puneah. You can meet them both."

A smile slips across her lips. "I'd love to." She goes out of the room and comes back a moment later. "When are you expecting Mina?"

"Anytime."

Her gaze flits to Wilric, her expression lighting, though it doesn't stay long. I wonder what happened between them while I was gone. Nothing too serious, I hope. I'd hate for her to get in trouble for being too close to him and the pain it would bring to them both. Some things aren't right.

"Things have been a lot quieter without you around," she says.

"I'm sure you are loathe to see me back."

"On the contrary. I like things lively."

I can't help it. I chuckle. "Is that what you call it? *Lively?*"

"It's a fitting description."

"I suppose it is. No attacks on the palace while I was gone?"

Her gaze slides to the side. "I wouldn't say that. Just nothing like what we've had to deal with when you're here."

That's to be expected. Maybe not everyone knows I left. Or maybe people aren't always after me, but something else? "How has your training been coming along?"

Out of the corner of my eye, I see Wilric smile.

Jem frowns. "I'm not as good as you yet."

I laugh. "I've been training my whole life. Of course, you're not as good as me yet. But are you getting better?"

"I think so." She doesn't sound certain.

"Excuse me for saying something, but she is improving every day." Wilric holds his position despite joining the conversation.

"I'm glad to hear it. I'm afraid the days ahead won't get any easier, and knowing how to protect yourself will be vital." It had better not come to that, but she's already been under the line of fire while with me, and that makes her training a good choice.

"I hope you don't mind, but I've been teaching the other ladies-in-waiting some of what I learned."

"Mind? Not at all. We should get them out there, learning with the guards, so at the very least they can defend themselves. And those who are training to be queen after me should be trained as well. It's a precarious position to place yourself in. They need to be protected by more than just guards." Why didn't I think of this sooner? "Would you be willing to oversee that?"

"I would be happy to."

On impulse, I add. "Wilric can help you. You seem to get along well."

Her cheeks turn a becoming shade of pink. Wilric stares

straight at my wall, like I didn't say a word. Perhaps I shouldn't have, but it came out.

A servant announces Venda. She comes in the room, Puneah trailing at her side. The large animal comes straight for me.

"She has taken to you," Venda says with her strange accent.

Just what I wanted.

"I've never seen such a beautiful creature," Jem says. "I can't believe filas are real."

"Rare, but yes, very real," Venda says.

"Can I pet her?" Jem asks.

"That is up to Puneah."

Jem licks her lips. "Does she bite?"

"Let her smell you." I unwillingly pet the sleek creature. She has gotten to me somehow, though we haven't spent much time together.

Jem sticks out her hand, and Puneah ignores her, instead putting her head down on my lap. When Jem's hand connects with Puneah's head, Puneah snorts but otherwise does nothing.

"She's so soft," Jem says.

She's a pain. If she gets any more comfortable on me, she's going to start drooling. Or biting. One of the two, and it's difficult to say which.

A servant announces Mina, and Venda excuses herself, leaving Puneah behind. Great. Now I really hope the fila doesn't bite. There'll be no one around to control it.

"Your Maj—" Mina's eyes grow wide as she looks at the fila. "What is that?"

"My new pet." There's a note of irony to my words. I don't care.

"So the rumors are true? You got a f—fila?"

"Don't be scared. She hasn't bitten anyone." Yet.

Mina nods but doesn't take her eyes off the creature. "You wanted to see me?"

"Yes. On my travels, I learned more about other countries, as you can see." I motion toward Puneah, whose head is still on my lap, her eyes now closed. "I'd like to know more about them. What do you know of Faner?"

"Not as much as you'd like, I'm afraid."

"What do you mean by that?"

"For one thing, I had no idea the country had filas. And if the woman I just saw is any indication of what other Faners look like, I had no clue that they were…"

"Shimmery?" I ask.

"Yes, that would be a good way to put it." She sighs. "I know more about Torhun and Insti than I do Faner."

Hm. "Is it true what they say about Torhun? Is it really run by a beast?"

She shifts in her chair. "I haven't met him personally, but from my intelligence, yes, he is half-beast, half-man."

"What does that even mean?" Jem asks.

"I—I don't know for sure. I think it means he's part of an actual beast, and not only a horrid person, though they say his temper is something fierce."

"Magic." It's all I can say. What else would cause someone to be half-beast?

"Assuredly," Mina says.

"What else can you tell me about Faner from what you've heard?"

"They don't have the resources we do—the mines of precious gems, stones, iron, and the like. They do have a lot of farmland. It's what keeps them alive. Their climate is supposed to be similar to ours."

Puneah purrs. I don't want to touch the beast, but something about that sound makes me feel like a child again. "Any reason for them to spy on us?" I ask.

She shrugs. "Difficult to say. They may want our resources, but there's not an easy way to get them with the mountains in the way. They'd have to either find a better way through or make the mountain pass wider. As it is, only one person can get through at a time, and it's a narrow fit."

It's something I'd like to see for myself but not today. "Any questions, Jem?"

"None."

"Then I would like to thank you for taking the time to come," I tell Mina. "If you think of anything further about our neighboring countries that would be helpful to know, please let me know."

"Of course, Your Majesty." She curtsies and leaves the room.

Jem and I discuss her fighting techniques, which is so second nature to me that I'm free to use my mind on other things. What are other countries like? Is there a benefit to widening the pass and opening communications with them, or is my country safer with it being so hard to go from one place to another? I wish being royalty came with knowing what to do.

CHAPTER 32

IT'S about time for the council meeting, but I'm savoring time with Nash—even if we're only talking politics. Puneah is in the sitting room with us, sleeping at my feet while I grudgingly let her.

When there's a break in the conversation, I say, "I have an idea. I'm not sure how it would work, though. I realized when we were traveling around Valcora that the cities don't trade with each other much, though each city has something to offer the others. Do you think we could increase trade? Make more tax money off it perhaps?"

He regards me thoughtfully. "I never thought about it, but yes. It could potentially work. The cities could benefit from each other."

"If it gets people to trade more, we might actually be able to make more money from taxes. If this works, we might be able to lower the taxes on the Kurah and still have plenty."

"They would love that, and it'd be good for the country as a whole. I say you should do it. Not because they threatened you, but because it's the right thing to do."

I hesitate.

"What's the problem?" His voice is full of concern.

This is Nash. I promised to be honest. If only it wasn't so hard. "After all the mistakes I've made, I'm worried about making another one."

He takes my hand, sending a wave of heat up my arm. Puneah gets up from her nap and sniffs the link between Nash and me. He chuckles. "I thought this fila looked fearsome the first time I saw her, but now I'm thinking she's sweeter than a kitty."

I roll my eyes. "She's certainly something."

"You don't like her?"

"I don't know her."

"Fair enough." He gives my hand a squeeze. "As for your concern—everyone makes mistakes. It's a part of life."

"The First Queen told me something similar before, but it's hard to change my thinking. Hard to believe my bad choices don't affect the country."

"First off, this isn't a bad choice. It will be good for the people and help them thrive. But even if it doesn't end up doing that, don't you think it's worth the risk of trying?"

Is it? I put all the conviction I can muster into my words. "It is."

"Then let's do it." He stands, tugging me gently to my feet.

Puneah takes a twirl around my legs.

"Thank you," I say.

He grins, looking more like his old self than I've seen in a while. "For you, anything."

Our hands part, and the world is colder without his touch. Together but separate, we head toward the council room, guards surrounding us as soon as we leave the room. Puneah follows at my side. I'm getting used to her presence.

That doesn't mean I like it.

When we get to the council room, everyone is already present. Nash takes my right side, and I sit, the others following suit after me. I don't wait. I jump right into my idea of opening up trade between cities, explaining it the same way I did to Nash.

I pause to see if any of them have something to say.

Timit is the first to speak, unsurprisingly. "It hasn't been done in my lifetime, but I think it's a good idea."

Wait, what?

If Timit thinks it's a good idea, maybe I'm on the wrong track.

"I like it as well," Kada says. "Though it does bring about questions, like—how are we going to get them to trade more? What if they don't want to? Are the road conditions good enough to facilitate such a venture?"

"These are all things we can easily look into," Nash says.

"I believe it would be good progress for our country," Sidle says.

"As do I," Jaku adds.

Soon, everyone is agreeing. It's like I've entered an alternate dimension, where the council forgot how to argue.

When everyone's had their say, I ask, "How do we make this happen?"

Puneah chooses that moment to put her head on the table and growl. Several squeals sound. I roll my eyes. Drama queen.

After we discuss opening trade, I tell them about probably purchasing the mine from Coplo.

"It would bring more income and jobs," Timit rumbles.

Am I winning him over to my side?

"I agree," Mina says.

Others concur.

"Once I have the details from Coplo, I will let you know," I say.

We finish up business, and I end the meeting. Everyone is waiting for me to leave so they can go. I stand.

"Before you go," Kada says, stopping me, "I wanted to let you know there's to be a country dance tonight to honor your return."

Her words make me feel lighter. Freer. That is, until I

remember what happened last time I went out and danced among the people. I saw Daros. While he be there this time?

Doesn't matter. I'm going anyway. Guards will be there, and I have my skills. Everything will be fine. "Perfect. Thank you for setting it up."

She bows her head. "It was no trouble."

Better yet, with a country dance, I won't have to dress fancy.

CHAPTER 33

IT'S ALMOST time to leave for the dance, but I find myself wandering the palace. There's a place I want to visit. I pass by halls and décor that's finer than anything I knew before I came here. I wind my way toward the back of the palace, windows facing the tombs that are almost as big as the palace themselves. I continue my journey, trying not to think of death. There's been enough of that in my life as it is. When I arrive at the chalice room, I tell my guards to wait outside.

"I should come with you," Wilric says.

"I'll be fine."

He purses his lips. "At least let me check out the room."

"Very well."

It takes him several minutes, but eventually he returns, proclaiming it free from threats.

The room is cold and dim in the drawing day with no torches lit. I'm an eerie presence in the mirrors surrounding the room. Like a ghost.

And perhaps I am a ghost of the person I was before, transformed into some new being that even I don't understand yet.

There's no sound as I slip through the room. It's so different than the first time I came running in. Thoughts and feelings rush through me. Panic me. I shake my head.

I am not the person I was then.

Doesn't stop the memories from coming.

I shove them away as best I can and make my way to the chalice. It sits on the pedestal, almost glowing. Maybe it is. I don't understand the magic contained within it.

And yet, I keep drinking it.

Thoughts try to flood me, but I don't dare acknowledge them. Instead, I run my fingers across the names chiseled onto the pillar. They automatically appear when someone dies from drinking the Mortum Tura. The names are tiny, filling all sides of the chest-high pillar. There must be thousands upon thousands of names here.

So many women died. Had their life taken from them because they wanted to be queen. How many of them were desired to rule and to do good for their country? Not all, I'm certain, but it stands to reason that many on this list would have done a good job.

I know the First Queen said this was the only way to make it work, but it is barbaric.

Besides, how many queens have taken this country to ruin? I remember someone once saying all queens turn out cruel. That the power gets to them, and they become hungry for it—eager for a way to get what they want instead of what's best for the people.

What power does the Mortum Tura hold that prevents the queens who've been crowned from turning? The First Queen's presence feels near. I wish I could ask her more about it— thoughts that I didn't think on previously, things that should have crossed my mind. I should, tonight.

Before I realize what I'm doing, I grab the chalice and guzzle the Mortum Tura until it's two thirds of the way gone. I slam it back down on its pedestal. It tastes so good. Like sweetness and power.

But I never wanted power.

Even now, I'd gladly trade it to someone else, but not if it meant my death. Which it will, and there's no guarantee that the new queen will want to take care this country. Queen Deedra was example enough of that.

I wipe my mouth with the back of my hand, trying not to think about the power pulsing through my veins and ignoring the fact that all the mirrors around me are lighting up with the glow of the Mortum Tura.

The magic coursing through me is almost like a living thing. What can I do with it? Is there something that could help me or my people? There has to be some use to all this magic, or there's no point in continuing to drink it.

The First Queen should know. I add that to my list of questions. Then again, maybe I should be looking myself. Using my resources. The library will have information on magic. Books that can help me understand it better. If I can understand it, perhaps I can help the people understand it better too.

A noise comes from behind me. I whirl around, draw my daggers, and press them against the neck of the woman behind me. A guard stands next to her.

"Who are you? What are you doing here?" I ask.

Her voice shakes. "I was sent for the chalice, for the country dance."

I withdraw my blades, pretending like her startling me was nothing. "Of course. Take it."

She curtsies before taking the chalice and setting it on a serving board she held. Without looking at me, she hurries from the room.

I glance back at the pedestal, with all those names carved on it. Women who shouldn't be forgotten, yet most are probably no more than a name carved on the stone.

I will remember them.

CHAPTER 34

"Where have you been?" Inkga asks.

She must be getting comfortable if she's willing to talk to me like that. "Around."

"Well, *around* isn't going to earn you a bath before festivities. We'll have to skip it."

I shouldn't have taken so long. A bath would have been nice. I've gotten used to having deliciously warm water in a large tub. It was worth missing it this time, though. I needed to think on those names.

"At least it's a country dance and not a formal one," she continues. "Preparing you for it will be a lot easier than if we had to do everything fancy."

She motions to my chair in front of my vanity, and I take a seat and glance at her through the mirror as she runs her fingers through my hair.

"It's growing so fast. I might be able to put braids in it. Then we can pin up the ends."

"Whatever you think is best." Blades know she understands a lot more about this than I do.

She moves the brush through my hair. "One day, you may have

an opinion on this."

"And take over your job?" It would be less to worry about than being the queen, if nothing else.

She laughs. "I don't think you'll ever replace me."

"I'm glad you have such confidence." My words are dry.

"Not as much as you think I have, but it's definitely increased since you gave me this position." She moves her fingers deftly through my hair, pulling and twisting in ways I can tell will make flattering results.

"Giving you this position was one of the smartest things I've done," I say.

"I don't know about that, but I appreciate the position."

"How are your parents?"

"They are good. Content."

"I'm glad to hear it. I wouldn't want to have people in my employment unhappy."

"You know, you can't make everyone happy." She finishes with my hair.

I swirl around in my seat to face her. "Maybe not, but I can do my best."

She smiles. "And I'll do my best to help you."

We continue to talk as she helps me pick out a plain yet beautiful dress that will help me stand out, but not too much. After I'm ready, she brings out a simple tiara that is enough to make me known as the queen, but more subdued than something I would wear to a more formal event.

I glance in the mirror. The silver lines shine against my hair, settling in perfectly along my braids. My eyes are bright with excitement, and I have a grin on my face. If now's not a good time to make my entrance, I don't know what will be.

"I'm ready," I say.

Julina, who's been silent in the corner of my room, moves to my door and opens it, then goes through first to make certain a problem didn't arise while I was getting ready. She comes back and motions for me to go ahead of her.

When I go out of my sitting room, Jaku and the other guards are waiting for me, along with my ladies-in-waiting. They are all dressed more simply than I'm used to, with narrower skirts and less lace and beading.

They curtsy at my entrance, and I take my place in the middle of the group, anxious to see what tonight will bring. My wish is for joy and happiness to my people. And if I'm lucky, to Nash.

We walk a ways down the hall and turn a corner to find Mother and Father headed toward us. They give a bow and join our group, Mother talking faster than I can keep up with.

Father is silent as usual. Sometimes I think I'm more related to him than her. He's quiet and can stalk into a room. He seems to think deeply, though I should strive to be more like Mother—friendly and outgoing. It's hard to open myself up to that when I'm not sure it's me. I have to push myself to expand into who I need to be.

Nash is waiting by the doorway of the palace, along with the rest of the council. I wasn't certain they were going to make it, but I suppose it's something they're required to do. They bow to me, and even after I tell them to rise, I wonder about them. Are they going to continue working with me. I ignore it for now. There will be time to think on it later.

The thought of him will not be ignored, though.

Nash.

His presence burns bright against the others. I let my gaze flitter to him. He gives a hint of a smile, and then we're off, and I can't pay him any more attention. I smile and wave at everyone, but my mind stays with him. With how much I want him and how it can never be. With the way I care for him—love him—and how my duty will always come before us.

We pass through the open portcullis, and I watch the crowd gathered on both sides of the road. As I pass, they bow, then rise and follow us.

We go deeper into the heart of the city. It doesn't take long to walk there, but the procession grows slower the farther we go from the crowd. The road is full of people, and as it opens up into an open square, I hear the pounding of a drum. Then all goes silent.

Everyone looks to me with eager eyes, except for my guards, who stay vigilant. It's times like this, when great things are expected of me, that I hate being the queen.

What do I say? I should have thought of this beforehand. I can let them know I care and that I'm trying. Is it enough?

"Thank you all for coming. I'm grateful to be back in the city and among you. While I was out on my travels of the country, I saw much. One thing I want to relate to you is that I plan to open trade among the cities. As such, I will be lowering taxes on goods traded between cities to encourage movement." And hopefully the council doesn't get upset with me for not talking with them about this in detail.

Someone claps, then another and another, until the whole square and beyond is full of cheering. Maybe I'll get this thing right—at least sometimes.

I raise a hand to quiet the crowd, though it takes some time to reach the outer edges of the crowd. Once they're fairly silent, I encourage everyone to dance.

The square becomes alive with life, the drum pounding out a rhythmic beat, while a vilka is strummed. People clear out of the center of the square, making room for dancers. Even some of my council members join them. There are smiles on everyone's faces. Except Nash's.

He stands, staring straight ahead, ignoring me as I'm trying to ignore him.

There's an energy between us, though. Something almost tangible, like a string that hums, going from him to me, pulling me toward him. To notice him. To touch him. To feel him.

But I'm stuck staring at the dancers.

I pretend the connection's not there. That I'm not being called to him.

A new song starts up. Someone taps their foot, and others follow until the sound reverberates through the air. The drums pound with the rhythm, the vilka playing a tune. The crowd dances, and I join in from where I'm standing, stomping my foot and clapping.

Energy fills me and brings the music through me, making me smile. I glance at Jaku, but he's watching the area around me with the rest of the guards. Pretending I'm not alone in my dancing, I continue.

* * *

EVERYTHING SETTLES DOWN, the music stopping for the night, though the crowd has yet to thin. They're probably waiting for me to leave.

A servant weaves her way through the crowd toward me, holding the board with the Mortum Tura on it. Time to drink.

Before she can get to me, a man crashes into her and grabs the chalice. My hand goes to the hilt of my dagger as he holds the chalice up in the air.

"We will not bow to a queen who ignores the Kurah's demands. If she doesn't give into us, she will perish."

Two daggers are out now, my guards moving around me, Julina and Wilric keeping close. Jaku herds me back, which is probably the smartest course of action. If I'm not here, the crowd will be in less trouble. Before I can take more than a few steps, a group of Kurah comes running up behind us, blocking our path out.

"Please return to your homes in peace," I call out.

"We will not back down until you are dead," a woman says.

The crowd that's not richly dressed is fleeing, heading away from the coming fight. My guards and Nash have their swords drawn. The rest of my council isn't in sight. The girl who brought the Mortum Tura out makes a grab for it, but the man shoves her to the ground.

"You will not treat others so disrespectfully," I yell. I hold up a dagger. "Leave now or face my wrath."

"We will not retreat." He holds the chalice high in the air.

I let my dagger fly and land in his wrist. The chalice falls out of sight.

The rest of the Kurah rush at us. I say to my guards, "Try to disarm them and not hurt them."

None of the attackers even reach me. They come at the guards in big groups, but without the training the guards have, they are quickly disarmed.

I stalk my way to the nearest one. "Who is your leader?"

He jumps up, pulls a knife out of his pocket, and tries to stab me with it. I easily block it and take the knife, then hand it to my closest guard without taking my eyes off the man. "Tell me who your leader is now."

He has the decency to look scared but still says nothing.

I snarl in disgust. "Did you think you'd be able to attack me and win? It's not going to happen. Now, tell me who yo—"

I'm shoved aside, a body going heavy on me as I smack against the ground. What in all the blades is going on?

The body on top of me is limp. I push it over to the side to find everything in chaos. I glance down at the body to discover Jaku has an arrow coming out of his shoulder and blood dripping from a wound on his head. He's out cold.

There's no time to help him, though, if I'm to live through this and help others. The best option for Jaku is for me to fight and then give him aid. He saved my life. It's my chance to return the favor—if he can last that long.

I jump to my feet, daggers raised. Guards are fighting all around me. Julina and Wilric are closest, but even with all their skills, they are being overwhelmed. A woman with a scar down the right side of her face sneaks past their defenses and comes at me with a dagger of her own.

I dodge her thrust toward my stomach and dive for her. My blade sinks into her thigh, making her howl with rage. I yank my blade back out, ignoring the wound. She pulls out two more daggers and comes at me despite her injury.

We move like we're dancing, dodging in and out. I sway around while I keep close to Jaku to protect him from her. She might not want to do him harm, but I'm not going to chance it. He's been there for me unlike so many haven't. The least I can do is protect him.

There's the scent of blood in the air. The sound of metal hitting against metal as blades clash. It's difficult to tell which side is winning and which is losing while focusing in on my opponent.

While trying not to die.

She thrusts. I block it, knocking her wrist with my fist and diving in for a hit. Before I make contact, her second blade knocks mine off course.

"Who is your leader?" I call out to distract her more than to get answers.

She sneers, throwing her dagger toward my middle. I fling it to the side with my own, leaving her with one less weapon.

"You'll never win." She throws her second dagger while pulling out another from her boot. I block this one as well, sweat beading on my forehead.

The sounds of battle narrow in. I can do this. I jump into the fight, letting my limbs move with the remembered attack. She fights back, but her gaze loses its confidence. I'm gaining on her, and she knows it.

"Tell me who your leader is, and we can end this now." I don't stop moving as the words come out.

She blocks my left weapon but misses my right as it cuts into her shoulder. She gasps aloud, cursing my name. Before she can react further, I knock the dagger from her hand and press mine to her neck.

"Who is your leader?"

Her eyes water, but her lips press together in a way that says she's not talking.

"If you won't talk, one of your friends my guards are fighting will," I say.

Her brows crease, but she doesn't say a thing. I've got to get to Jaku and stop the bleeding—bring a healer to him who knows what to do, not deal with this piece of junk that tried to kill me. Her gaze darts behind me—the only warning I get. I whirl around to find a huge man with his sword lifted above his head, about to bring it down at me.

I strike like a snake, sneaking in and getting him in the armpit before he can bring his blade down. He howls in pain, but I don't have time to see how much damage I did. A blade is pressed to the middle of my back.

"Say *goodbye* to this world," the woman behind me says.

She's going to stab me in the back. I shove my elbow into her stomach and knee the man in front of me in the groin, before turning on her. I snatch the dagger out of her hand and jam the flat side of the blade against the side of her head.

She grasps her head but doesn't fall. One of my guards grabs her by the wrists and ties her up while I turn my attention back to the man. He's on the ground, another of my guards over him.

I lean over, adding my blade to his neck. "Who is your leader?"

His bottom lip trembles like a scared child's. "I—I don't know."

"Who do you take directions from?" I ask.

"A Kurah in a cloak. That's all I know. Please, spare me."

I curl my lip in disgust. Before I can get a word in, an arrow flies through the air and punctures his lung. I glance toward where the perfect shot came from, only to see the faint flash of a brown cloak disappearing into the night.

"Guards, after him," I yell. Two of my guards break off for him, but the rest stay behind. "What are you all doing? Go after that person."

"Forgive me, Your Majesty," Wilric says with a bow. "We can't leave you unprotected while there are so many attackers out. We need to get you back to the palace."

I growl. "What about Jaku?"

I glance to my side, where he's lying on the ground, another guard attending him. The arrow is still in his shoulder, but he's awake. Sort of. Blinking heavily, at least. That's a good sign.

"He'll be taken care of," Nash says. "He'd want for you to get out of here, away from the danger."

Danger. That's all that ever surrounds me. "Very well. Make certain he's well cared for. Send a runner for a healer. Grab the prisoners, and let's go to the palace." Though I don't want to leave Jaku, Nash is right. Jaku would want me to. Not only that, but by leaving him, I'm also taking the troubles with me.

If only I knew where the problems are coming from.

CHAPTER 35

As soon as we enter the palace, I holler at servants to send more guards back for Jaku and the others, then I yell for prisoners to be taken to the dungeons—except for the one who seems most compliant. That one should be taken to a room and interrogated. After that, I send even more guards out to search for the archer or archers. Chances are we lost whoever it was, but I can't be certain without trying.

If only I'd been a little faster. A little stronger.

I should have been training with Nash more. Doing something to make myself better besides regular exercises. My skills are growing weaker without something to challenge them daily. No use worrying about it now.

I turn to the nearest servant. "Send word as soon as you have an update on Jaku."

If he dies on my watch, saving my life, I'll never be able to forgive myself. I just have to go and put myself in danger.

No. It's not my fault. It's the Kurah's.

They are the ones who attacked. They and some well-trained assassins. Between the two, it could be his undoing. It won't be mine.

The servant bows and scurries off. Everyone hurries around me, like a storm is brewing and I am the force behind it.

"Nash?"

"Yes, Your Majesty?"

"Take me to the interrogation room. You can come in, if you'd like, but we're going to find out who's at the bottom of this."

"Right this way." He turns and heads down a hall that leads toward the dungeon. I follow him, my many guards surrounding me. There are several more than usual, like even in the palace they don't trust that I'm safe.

Not that they should. I've never been safe, no matter where I go.

Nash leads me through the halls until we reach a door near the dungeon. A guard stands on either side, and Nash says a word to them. He then opens the door and proceeds to lead me inside, where two more guards watch over a man sitting on the sole chair in the room.

It's dark in here, with no windows or any light except for a lantern held by one of the guards. The man sitting on the chair isn't one I recognize from the fight. He must have been taken down by one of my guards. He has a big chin and nose and small eyes that are too far apart. His expression says he doesn't want to talk to me, but there's a hint of fear in those tiny eyes.

I pull out my dagger and use it to clean under my fingernails. I take my time, though what I want is to scream at him to give me answers. Once I finish with one hand, I move on to the other. I don't have long nails, but the process is what matters.

When I'm done, I slide the dagger back into its hilt with a snick. The man before me has beads of sweat dripping down his forehead.

"What was your mission, and who ordered you to do it?" I ask in my calmest yet most sinister voice.

The man's response is shaky. "You can't make me talk."

I let a grin creep across my lips. "Are you sure about that?"

He whimpers.

"I see my reputation precedes me, so let's make this easy. You give me answers, and I won't be forced to hurt you." I wouldn't, though he doesn't need to know that.

His chin quivers, but he clamps his mouth shut. Doesn't want to talk but is scared not to. Maybe he needs a little nudge. I pull my dagger back out and almost place it on one of his fingers, but that reminds me too much of Nash and what he went through. Instead, I place it under his chin, the tip pointed up. "It would only be too easy to leave you with a hole in the bottom of your mouth." I pull the blade away but keep it out. "Did the Kurah hire you?"

He darts his gaze from me to the guards and back.

"We know the answer, so you might as well admit it," I say.

"They did."

"Good answer. And who—specifically—was it?"

He licks his lips. "I don't know."

I slide my blade against his neck. "What do you mean you don't know?"

"Please. I'll tell you. I would, anyway, because there's not much to tell."

I don't take the dagger away. "Tell me."

He swallows, his Adam's apple bobbing against the metal. "The man who hired me was wearing a cloak with the hood up. I didn't see his face."

As much as I'd like to think otherwise, I believe he's telling the truth.

"What color was the cloak?"

"Brown."

Same as before. "Did you notice any jewelry or other clothing?"

"Nothing. It was dark, and he was hidden within the folds of his cloak."

Drat. I'm going to get no further information.

I storm from the room, Nash on my heels. Once the door is closed, I say, "I want you to interview all the Kurah who attacked us. Find out who organized them."

He gives a jerky nod, eyes haunted. "Consider it done."

Is he strong enough to do this? "Are you certain?"

His voice lowers. "Anything for you, My Queen."

Warmth blossoms through me, though there's no time to dwell on it. "Thank you. I'll interview the rest of the mercenaries and see what I can find out."

We part ways, though my heart says that we should stay together. I know that we need to do this.

It takes hours and hours, but all I get from those I can get to talk is the same answer. Two hold out, refusing to say a thing, but the others all say the man who hired them was hooded and cloaked, hiding his features. Male, medium build, in a nondescript brown cloak. That's the best description I can get out of them. It's not nearly enough. That could describe almost half of the population.

I stalk through the halls, ignoring my guards as I head toward the interrogation room Nash should be working at. He's leaning against the wall, by the door, expression so neutral I can't tell what he's thinking.

"Any luck?" I ask.

He runs a hand through his short hair, fingers shaking. "No. Everyone I talked to heard a rumor from someone else in this prison. The one woman who didn't hear it from another Kurah said she heard it from a man cloaked and hooded in brown."

"Let me guess. Medium build?"

"Yes."

I refrain from punching the wall, but only just. It would do much greater damage to me than I would to the brick. "This is useless. Someone wants me dead or to give in to them, and we don't know who. The Kurah are too well-organized. Everything is going far too smoothly for them. I don't know what to do."

"I'll keep searching for answers." His voice is soft, calming my rage.

I want to go to him, to find solace in his touch, but there are too many guards around. "Why don't you go rest for the night? It's been a long day. Hopefully, we'll have more answers for you in the morning. In the meantime, you can get a clear head."

His eyes have dark circles under them, fraught with heavy blinks.

"I will, on the condition that you get some rest too. You need to sleep, to refresh yourself."

He opens his mouth, eyes fierce, but then they soften. "You're right. I'll try. But first let me walk you back and find out if there's any news on Jaku."

"Fair enough."

We head out toward my rooms. The stroll is companionable but silent. Though I'm frustrated and upset, being next to him is soothing, even if we can't touch. It doesn't take long to reach our destination. A servant is waiting outside the door.

Julina goes to check inside while the servant gives us a report on Jaku. "He's going to make it. The healer wants him to take it easy for a while, but Jaku is trying to get up and about. Says he needs to figure out why this attack happened and keep it from happening again."

Tension leaves me. He's going to be all right. "Tell him he's to rest, by order of the queen. He can get back to his job when the healer says he's well enough."

"Yes, Your Majesty. I'll try."

Try may be all any of us can do, but it's enough to ease my worries, if nothing else. As long as he didn't die saving my life and is going to heal well, I can be fine with him trying to get back to work.

I excuse the servant and glance at Nash. He gives me a bow,

and as I go into my rooms, I turn to see him talking to one of the guards.

"Your rooms are clear, Ryn," Julina says, "but your parents are in there, waiting for you."

How long have they been waiting? It doesn't matter. There's nothing I can do to change it. "Very well."

I move into my rooms. Julina stays outside, but Wilric follows me in and places himself in an out-of-the-way corner. It's warm in here, the fire lighting up the room against the dark night. I barely have time to register that much before Mother is almost on me, tears streaming down her face.

"We heard you were almost killed again. I couldn't handle it if something happened to you."

"I'm fine. Nothing to worry about." I've been gone for much longer than I meant to—especially for not learning anything.

"We had to make certain you're all right."

I glance at Father, who's waiting behind her. He nods but doesn't get a chance to speak before his wife continues.

"I've never seen so many attackers at once. I don't think you should go out anymore. Let the people come here to see you. Don't put yourself at risk of being hurt again."

My immediate instinct is to snap that I will do what I want to, but then I realize she's only trying to protect me. If it wasn't so annoying, it'd be nice to have someone thinking and caring about me. "I know you're trying to help, but I must do what's needed of me as leader of this country. Between my skills and those of my guards, I'll be fine."

She wrings her hands. "If you think that's best."

"I do. But I appreciate your concern."

She goes silent and moves to the window to look outside.

I walk deeper in the room, facing Father. He gives me a commiserating look. Whatever he feels about his wife, he knows how over the top she can be.

On the other hand, she does care.

There's a knock at the door. I turn to glance at who is coming in. There's a sharp pain in my back. I cry out and dive forward while grabbing my daggers. I whirl around, ready to face an enemy.

Father—Carver stands in front of me, knife drawn, wet with my blood.

CHAPTER 36

EVERYONE IS FROZEN, staring at that knife for a split second. Carver jumps toward me, but Wilric blocks him.

I'm too stunned to do anything other than watch as Wilric takes Carver down, ties him up, and calls out for other guards. Something drips down my back. I blink and force myself to move as the door is opened.

Guards pour in the room and surround me, Nash leading them. "What happened?"

Wilric glances up at me. "Are you all right, Your Majesty?"

It takes me a moment to reply, "Fine."

"Are you certain? You're rather pale."

I blink heavily. "I'm sure." I can barely feel the stinging in my back. The stinging in my heart is something else entirely.

Wilric hauls Carver to his feet with his hands tied behind his back and turns his attention to the guards. "He attacked Her Majesty."

One of the guards gasps. I can't take my eyes off Carver, who's hanging his head.

"Why did you do it?" Shillian—I can no longer think of her as

Mother—says between her sobs. How long has she been crying? "Our own daughter, and you attacked her. Why?"

Is this an act? Is she in on it too? Or is she an innocent bystander? Either way, I'm not sure I'll ever be able to trust her again.

I echo her question. "Why?"

Carver finally lifts his head, his eyes so haunted I flinch. "I had debt that needed to be repaid. He said killing you was the only way I could repay it."

"Who said?" I have a feeling I already know.

"Daros."

I clench my teeth. That man gets into my hair more than anyone should.

"You were willing to kill your own daughter to pay back a debt to Daros?" Wilric asks with venom in his voice.

Carver hangs his head again, shoulders sagging. "It was a lot of debt."

I fold my arms in front of my chest, not sure if I'm holding myself together or holding myself back. "You're despicable."

He hunches more.

Shillian comes around to face him, tears still streaming down her face, though the sobs have quieted. She smacks him across the face. "I thought you were done gambling when we had to give up our daughter. You're disgusting. I want nothing to do with you ever again."

He doesn't even have the decency to look up.

I nod to the closest guard. "Please take Shillian Nilmac and have her questioned."

She turns to me, despair smeared across her features. "You don't trust me?"

I hold her gaze. "I'm sorry. I can't."

She nods, though more tears drip. "I'll do what I can to earn your trust back." She turns and heads out the door, the guard following her.

"ARE YOU ALL RIGHT?" Wilric asks.

"Give me a moment, and then I'll worry about my back. It's not a big wound."

I return my attention to Carver. I feel like smacking him myself but refrain. "I'm going to ask you a few questions, and you're going to answer them honestly. All right?" I've had more than enough of this tonight, but I want answers now.

"I have nothing left to live for, anyway, now that I've failed."

I snarl. I can't believe this man is my father. "When was the last time you met with Daros?"

"Last night."

That's good news. If we can discover his location, we may recapture him. "And where did you meet with him?"

"Here, in the palace."

I'm too well-trained to gasp, and thankfully, so are my guards. Nash glances at me, eyes clouded with worry. I turn my focus back on Carver. "Where in the palace?"

He looks at me, his gaze earnest. "You won't find him if he doesn't want to be found. He's come to me as a guard, as a servant, and as a courtier. He's well-versed in disguises."

Which I should have guessed since he was the one who taught me that skill, though I haven't put it to much use. "Doesn't matter. Where did you last meet with him?"

He drops his head again. "In my rooms. He was dressed as a servant."

My back stings, but I push the pain aside and turn to Julina. "Organize a search throughout the entire castle. No one is above suspicion. No one."

"Consider it done, Your Majesty." She bows and rushes from the room.

"Any other questions for the prisoner, Your Majesty?" Wilric asks.

"No. Send him to the dungeons to await his fate."

Wilric passes him off to a skinny guard, who takes him away.

"The rest of you may leave," I say.

They filter from the room, leaving Wilric behind. I should have kept Julina around so I could sleep. Granted, I don't think I'll be able to sleep after all that's happened, though I'm exhausted.

Inkga should be here soon. I'll at least be able to change into something more comfortable to work out in. I pace the room, trying to decide what my next course of action should be. Was Daros in this castle the entire time? How is he getting away with blending in without being caught?

"My lady," Wilric says from his post in the corner. "Might I suggest that we get a healer for your back?"

It's still stinging, wet, and sticky. "Send for one."

He opens the door and calls a servant to send for the healer.

It's a scratch; it won't do much, though it would be nice to have it cleaned up.

Several minutes later, there's a knock on the door and a servant announces Inkga and the healer. They both enter, and Inkga comes straight to me while the unfamiliar healer sets down her things on the low table, her ample body taking up a good chunk of space.

"I heard you've been injured," Inkga says.

I wave away her concern. "I'm fine."

"The palace is going mad with the search for Daros."

"They'd better find him soon." I feel like raging but not at her. Part of me wants to be scared again. Part of me *is* scared, but I shove it down, letting my anger boil it away.

The healer comes over, pulls something out of her long sleeve, and presses it to Inkga's throat.

"What are you doing?" I glance at the dagger and then at the healer's eyes. Her familiar eyes.

Daros.

CHAPTER 37

"YOU HAVE an uncanny knack of living through everything I throw at you," Daros says. "Until now."

My heart is thrumming in my ears so loud I can barely hear him. "Leave Inkga out of this. She's done nothing to you."

"And give up my advantage? I don't think so."

In the corner, Wilric goes to pull out his sword, but Daros shoves the dagger farther against Inkga's neck. I hold out a hand to stop him. "We can't let Inkga get hurt."

Daros grins, the long hair appearing wrong against the thin face that doesn't match him or his body. With his free hand, he shakes off the wig, revealing thinning brown hair. His rounded body looks incongruous with the rest of him, as does the well-rounded bosom I know isn't his.

"What do you want from me?" I ask to distract him so I can think of a plan.

"I want you dead."

So he can put someone else on the throne and control them, something he'll never be able to do with me again, even if it means giving up Inkga's life. I work hard not to gaze into her eyes. To ignore the fear and pain in them. To ignore that same fear and pain in me.

"Even if you kill me, there will be others who stand in your way," I say.

"I haven't come all this way to lose. Hold out your hand."

I hold my head high. "Why should I?"

"Because if you don't, I'm going to kill your little friend here."

I try to think of something that will buy me time and give me a way to save her, but all I can think of is obeying—for now. I won't let him win this.

I hold out my hand. "There. Happy?"

He grins. "Quite." With movements like a snake, he darts out and stabs my palm with the hand not holding a dagger on Inkga.

"What was that?" I barely feel the pinprick.

"Your downfall."

Before he can say anything else, the door opens. Jem rushes in the room and halts when she sees the scene. But it's enough.

Daros glances her way, and I slam my hand across his wrist, knocking the dagger out of his hand while at the same time pulling Inkga toward me. I shove her behind me, and Wilric is there with his sword.

Daros blocks Wilric with his dagger and pulls out a sword from his voluminous robes. Jem backs into a corner, calling for more guards, and pulls a dagger from her skirt. They pour in the room, Nash with them, but before they can get to us, Daros stabs Wilric.

Wilric puts a hand to his stomach, where the wound is bleeding. His face is going pale. I put my dagger to Daros's neck as Wilric falls to the ground. The guards point their blades at Daros, and Jem runs to Wilric, Nash right behind her.

Nash calls out, "Are you all right, Ryn?"

"Fine. How's Wilric?"

Nash kneels on the ground next to Wilric and looks him over.

He doesn't have to say anything; I can read it in his eyes. The wound is fatal, even if Wilric is still grasping onto life.

I press the tip of my weapon into Daros's neck, ready to make the killing blow.

"I wouldn't do that if I were you." Daros's voice is calm. Certain.

I hesitate. It's probably another trick to keep him alive. But there's nothing he could do with so many guards around him. "Take his sword and dagger."

Two guards grab them. I expect him to put up a fight, but he just stands there. I move so I see his face. See what he's thinking. "Why shouldn't I?"

"Two reasons I think you'll find very interesting."

I press my blade harder against his neck. "And they are?"

He smirks and takes his time answering. "One—because I poisoned you."

CHAPTER 38

Nash yells, *"No."*

Jem tears off a part of her skirt and covers Wilric's stomach while glancing at me, eyes wide. A guard says, "I'm going for a healer." The rest talk over one another in a jumbled mess, keeping their swords on Daros. I wait, processing what's happening.

And Daros stands in the midst of it all, looking smug.

My brain kicks back into thought. "What poison?" I let the guards keep their swords on him as I pull the pouch off from around my neck.

"That won't do you any good," he says.

I don't care. I reach in and take a little of every antidote I have. They are bitter as they go down, but not nearly as bad as being poisoned. What poison is there left I'm not immune to? Only a few, and they're all minor.

Nash rushes past me and punches Daros in the face. "What is the antidote?"

"Ah, so we care for our little queen, do we?" Daros chuckles, blood streaming from his nose.

Nash shakes him with a growl. "I swear, if you don't tell me what poison it is, I will make your life more miserable than your death."

"It's simple—something I developed recently. If it doesn't kill her, it will leave her drained of her strength and muscle tone, rendering her useless."

I clench my teeth, trying to keep my emotions in. Nash doesn't hold back; he punches Daros again, the smack echoing through the room. Daros grunts, but the smile doesn't leave his face.

"Why would you do this?" I want to scream, but the words come out as a whisper. I know why, but it's still hard to fathom that it would actually happen.

"Simple. You didn't do what I wanted. I can't seem to kill you. The next best thing is to leave you maimed."

"You are a cruel, stupid man." My voice is tight.

"It's a pleasure, I assure you."

He's smug. Has he finally won the war?

I don't feel any weaker.

Except that's not true. The hand he pricked is limp. I try to make a fist with it, but it only goes halfway. I try again, pushing my fingers together as hard as I can. It won't work. No matter how much I try, I can't make a fist.

It's starting.

I'll never be able to protect myself again. Never be able to hold a dagger. Never be able to fulfill my duties as queen—if I manage to live.

Daros has won.

I realize Nash is watching me try to make a fist, his expression unreadable. He turns back to Daros, grabs his tunic with both hands, and shakes him. "How do we fix this?"

"It's simple." Daros brushes Nash's hands away. "You don't. Not without me. Not without giving into my control."

I'm going to be sick. "I'll never give in to you, so there's no point in keeping you around."

I raise my dagger with my good hand. The door bursts

open. It's a healer, accompanied by the guard who went to get him. The healer rushes to me, but I hold out a hand to stop him. "There's nothing you can do for me now. Help Wilric."

Thankfully, he doesn't question me. He moves next to Jem, peering under the red-soaked material. He shakes his head, and for a moment, I think he's going to give up. But then he gets to work.

I turn back to Daros. "For all your crimes, you will die."

Again, I raise the dagger.

"Remember I said I had two reasons." Daros is calm, which is more concerning than if he was upset. "I knew the first might not work against you, so I have a backup plan."

Of course he does. "I don't want to hear it. You've ruined enough with your venomous words."

"I didn't want to speak of it in front of so many, but you leave me with no choice. I believe you've met the First Queen."

There's a cold grip around my heart. The First Queen's presence draws near, and I can feel her interest. Her wonder. And maybe a little bit of something else. Something darker. Unless that's all me.

"We'll speak of this later." If I have a later. I turn to my guards, ignoring Nash's questioning glare. "Take him to a room with no windows and only a door to the hall and all of you stay with him until I come for him." Or die. But then Nash will take care of everything. I know he will.

As they move Daros away, I want to wipe the smug grin off his face, but there are more important things to deal with first. I hurry to Wilric's side and ask the healer, "What news do you have for me?"

He rubs the back of his hand on his forehead, not taking his eyes off of his patient. Jem does the same beside him, holding Wilric's hand. "I've given him some medicine that should help make him more comfortable, but..." The healer looks at me. "I'm sorry. For you all." His gaze switches to Nash, Jem, and finally lands on Wilric himself.

Wilric's pale face is scrunched together. His words are laced with pain. "At least I can say I died protecting my queen."

My chest squeezes so hard it hurts. "We can't just give up like this."

"It's all right Ryn," he says. "I'm at peace."

"Well, I'm not. There has to be something we can do. Some medicine or something better, like... magic." I turn to Nash. "Send a servant for Venda. Maybe she knows a spell that can help."

He bolts away.

"Now, can I please have a look at you, Your Majesty?" the Healer asks.

I wave away his concern. "Unless you know a way to stop a new poison that will kill me or weaken me if I live through it, there's nothing you can do."

"At least let me stitch up your back."

As if that will do me any good should I die. "After we get Wilric better."

He opens his mouth, and then seems to think better of it and snaps it closed.

My mind swirls with everything that's happened, but I force my focus on what's at hand. "Hold on, Wilric. Help is coming. You need to stay tough for me."

"Is that. An order. Your Majesty?"

"It is. I order you to stay alive until Venda gets here, and then you let her help you live."

"I'm afraid that's. One thing. I can't. Obey."

Jem breaks into a sob, resting her head against his shoulder. What transpired between the two of them while I was gone? They seem closer than ever, only now to be torn apart by death's embrace.

The door opens with a bang. Venda rushes in, Puneah trailing after, and I make room for her by his side. "Is there anything you can do for him?" I ask.

She doesn't reply, just waves two stones over his body. Her eyes are wide and wild, her cheeks almost rosy under the sheen of silvery skin. If I didn't know better, I'd say she looks mad. But then, maybe crazy is the only option we're left with.

She mutters something I can't make out under her breath. Jem glances up at her for a brief moment, hope shining in her eyes, before turning her gaze back to Wilric.

Venda continues moving the stones over him a moment before turning to me, her eyes wet. "I'm sorry. There is nothing I can do."

"Check. The queen," Wilric gasps out. "She's been. Poisoned."

Venda's gaze turns sharp. "With what?"

"I don't know. He said it was something new he'd made himself, but I don't know if that's true or not. It's supposed to kill me, and if it doesn't succeed at that, make me weak. I can feel it traveling up my arm."

All gazes in the room turn to my left arm. I want to hold it behind me so they can't see how limp it's hanging.

"I may be able to do something about that. Lie down." Venda's words are firm.

"Not until Wilric is taken care of." It seems silly to put my life before another's, even if I am queen.

"Now, or there may not be time. The longer the poison is in you, the more damage it will do." The sternness of her words takes me aback, but I do as she says. I lie on the floor next to Wilric, watching the life drain from him and taking my composure with it.

Tears leak from my eyes. "I don't want you to go. You've been a good protector and friend. Even more so to those I care about."

"I have to." His eyes close. "Make sure... my family knows... I love them."

"I will. You will be honored and remembered." The tears flow freely.

His chest gives one last heave. Then stillness.

Jem sobs, breaking down in a way I never thought I'd see. Nash clenches his jaw, his eyes wet.

Venda's voice pulls my attention back to her. "The poison has reached your heart."

The room goes silent with tension and sadness. Nash stands and moves just behind Venda, looking straight at me. Puneah stalks over to me, her tails twitching. She buries her head in my neck. For once, I don't want to swat her away but enjoy the comfort from one of the few places I can get it.

My vision darkens around the edges. I try to speak, but my mouth won't open. My body feels as if it's being torn apart, leaving me unable to control it. I want to scream and shout. Cry and rage. But I can do nothing.

Nothing.

Nothing.

CHAPTER 39

IT'S DARK.

Every muscle is weak.

I feel like I'm outside myself. Not connected to anything. Just floating...

Floating...

Floating...

Colors sparkle my vision—little pricks of reds, greens, yellows, and oranges, growing bigger and brighter.

Is this it? Have I... died?

I search for something—anything—to tell me that there's life. Breaths. Heartbeat. Blinking. They aren't there. None of it exists. Except...

The First Queen.

Her presence is near. I can't tell where she is; I only know she's here. Thinking. Probing.

I want to move. To talk and ask her questions. To find out what's going on. Am I feeling her in death or life? Has the poison affected me so much that I can't do anything? Has it taken me from life or left me maimed? Is this how I'm going to be forever?

Stuck in some sort of in-between state? I hope not because this is mental agony. I don't know how long I can stand it.

I continue that way. Drifting. Always drifting.

There are times I try to talk, to move or do anything, but nothing happens. Just more of the same. The entire time, the First Queen is here.

What does Daros know about her? What does he want to talk about? Maybe it will never matter. Maybe I'll be stuck in this place forever and will never find out.

Minutes, hours, days, months, *years* pass by in a panic of not being able to do anything. Despite how much time seems to pass, it all remains the same. A boring, unending splash of colors and nothingness.

Then finally, *finally*, something changes. The world blackens, slowly like a fog creeping in. With the darkness comes cold. Though it almost burns, it's so chilly that it's good to feel something. Anything. I embrace the pain and the low temperature.

Something happens so subtly I have to wonder how long it's been going on that I haven't been able to hear it. A faint sound. A mumble of something deep, followed by something light and airy. The grumbling grows louder, a faint tingling in my body.

My body. I can feel it. Faintly, but it's there. Maybe I cheated death. But what awaits me if I did so?

I try to blink. There's a flutter of light and darkness. I wince.

"She moved." Nash's voice. I'd recognize it anywhere.

Something soft moves against my hand and stays there. I blink again and groan, though it comes out faint.

"Ryn? Can you hear me? It's time to wake up."

"What happened?" My words sound cold and slurred. My mouth hurts from moving just that much.

"You passed out. Venda was able to keep you from death, but she wasn't sure how much damage would be done."

"Give yourself a minute, and you can try talking again." Venda's voice is smooth.

I force my eyelids open, feeling like there's a fifty-pound weight on each of them. The world is a blur of color. My breathing quickens. Am I back in that dreamless state? But then the world comes into view, and the panic recedes.

Above me, Nash and Venda are standing on opposite sides of the bed watching on. Puneah is at my hand on the bed, her head buried there. One question comes to me. "Wilric?"

Nash grimaces. "He's passed on."

Tears seep out of the corner of my eyes, but I can't brush them away. I can't even blink them away. The world smears before me. There's no way to control the flow of salty water out of my eyes. There's nothing I can do, and it only makes the tears come on harder.

I grit my teeth. It takes all my energy to do so and blink several times. I'm strong. I can handle death. It's something I'm familiar with. But life without strength? I don't know if I can take it.

"It's all right," Venda says. "Try and keep calm. I believe the poison has weakened you, despite my trying to stop it."

I steel myself to get the words out. "How long will I be like this?"

The faintest wrinkle appears between her eyebrows—something most people wouldn't notice. "I don't know," she says. Whatever the real answer is, I don't like it.

"Don't know, or don't want to tell me?"

She shakes her head. "Honestly, I'm not certain."

"What are the chances?" Nash asks, making me grateful he can ask what I can't.

Her words come out faint but audible. "That you may never regain your strength."

I let my eyelids close, not willing to keep them open. I'm grateful it's hard to move even my facial muscles. I don't want to show any emotion. Don't want to give away the torrent raging through me. For rage it does.

The pain is quick and intense. Daros injured me far greater

than if he killed me. He did me the ultimate harm. I've always been tough. Swift. Powerful.

And now, I'm nothing.

CHAPTER 40

A WEEK PASSES. Each day is agony as I try to work my muscles, to get them to obey me, but they're uncooperative. I get to where I can blink and talk, but the rest of my movements are slow and uncoordinated.

Others try to comfort me with the fact I still have life, but this is a nothingness like I've never experienced. A torment like no other. I never realized how much worse of a torture Daros could put me through than I've already been, but it happened.

Nash is the only one who doesn't try to coat things with sweet words and looks. He visits often, usually when others are about, to keep things proper since I'm stuck in bed. He doesn't require anything of me. Doesn't speak words that hurt to hear. He just stays near.

Inkga brought word only once that Shillian was begging to see me even though she'd been kicked out of the palace since being cleared by Jaku. I'm certain Shillian asked for me more, but I told Inkga I didn't wish to be informed of them. I don't want to think on the crimes of my parents right now. Or ever. I did ask about Jem though. My lady-in-waiting hasn't been by to see me since

Wilric died. My heart aches for her, but I haven't been able to talk to her. Not yet.

Puneah also visits often like Nash, and I'm finding her presence more soothing than I thought it would be. She never uses her teeth on me, but gives others ferocious looks. The servants avoid her, except Inkga, who acts like the fila isn't there.

She's here now, curled up on the side of the bed opposite of Nash.

"When is Wilric's funeral?" They are the first words I've spoken all day. I need to begin focusing on things outside myself, no matter how hard it is. I have a country to look after. Nash has been giving me reports, but I've done nothing with them. At least now I can focus on something important, though something that should never have been.

"It's tomorrow." The sorrow that laces his words is enough to make my heart ache.

"Best start dealing with things, then. Get Inkga, please."

The servant that was hiding in the corner hurries from the room to do my bidding. It's the first thing I've asked for since being confined to my bed. They've brought me food and drink, which I took, hoping it'd give me my strength back. None of it has worked. I'm as useless as never before.

Several quiet minutes later, Inkga comes in with the servant.

I say, "Help me sit up, please."

"Of course." There's no pity in her eyes, unlike the servant that came to assist her.

She's been by often too—the one to take care of me since I can't take care of myself. So few are allowed to touch me. Maybe that should change now that I have no strength, but I doubt it will.

Puneah slinks to the floor when I tell her to get down. I'm jostled about until I'm put in a sitting position, pillows behind me and all around me. Inkga wipes her brow. "What else can I help with, Ryn?"

Puneah jumps up beside me and curls into a ball at my side.

"Will you make sure that there's a way for me to attend Wilric's funeral?" Not that I want to go out in public looking like this, but I have to be there for him. He gave his life for me and made it so I could apprehend Daros, who is still locked up with several guards on a rotating schedule.

"Of course. I'll get right on it, unless you have something else you'd like me to do?"

"That would be perfect. Send Daros in with his guards after I speak with Jaku and Nash." I look at the other servant. "And you are dismissed. I'll send someone for you if I need you."

She curtsies. "Yes, Your Majesty."

They both leave. Nash says, "What are you going to do?"

"Something I should have done the moment I woke up. Take care of Daros." Even if I can no longer do it by my own hand.

I glance down at my motionless arms and legs that feel heavier than lead. A cringe works its way up, but I suppress it. I don't want to deal with that. More like, I can't.

We wait in silence, Nash's presence the only thing that reassures me. I don't know how I'm going to be the queen, but I know he'll do everything he can to help. Will it be enough?

Several minutes later, Jaku walks in. His shoulder is bandaged up and in a sling, but otherwise, he looks like his usual tough self. He doesn't say a thing about my condition, just gets right down to business. "Daros is waiting out in the hall. You want to see him now?"

"Yes, but first there's something I should tell you. Nash already knows, but I have to let you know too. I can't have Daros in here without some help, even if he's tied up. I don't trust him, but I trust you two. This may be hard to believe, but I assure you, it's true." I explain about the First Queen, and how she comes to me in dreamlike states and has been since I was crowned.

The only reaction he gives is a slight widening of his eyes.

"What do you think?" I ask.

"Daros knows of this, you say?"

"Yes, though I don't know to what extent or how he found out."

Jaku clenches the hilt of his sword with his good hand. "I will keep this honor bound between us, but it may do no good if Daros knows."

"You believe me, then?"

He hesitates. "I believe something strange is definitely going on. The Mortum Tura is magic, and it's true that we don't know much about it."

Not nearly enough. "Let's bring Daros in, unless you have any other thoughts?"

"I'll make certain he's well-tied up before bringing him in here. Since I'm injured, I'll only be of little use to you."

Nash stands and pulls out both a sword and a dagger. "He'll never again touch her if I have anything to say about it."

Jaku gives him a nod before leaving my room. Waiting for Daros is torture. Each moment seems like a lifetime. I realize I'm tying to pinch my fingers but they're barely moving. I want to growl in frustration but work to keep myself calm. To prove he can't intimidate me no matter what's to come.

But the fear is still there.

Then again, so is the rage.

The door opens. The guards surround Daros, bringing him into the room. They pull up a chair and tie him to it, though his wrists and ankles are chained together. Jaku and Nash flank him, swords out.

To the rest of the guards, I say, "You may go."

They leave.

Daros has a smug smile, his dark eyes not leaving mine. "You wanted to see me, girl?"

My old fear bubbles up at that name. I shove it down. I'm not that person anymore. "You know what I want," I say.

"It'd be much easier to speak with you without these chains on."

"It'd be even easier for my men to chop off your head."

The smile dims but doesn't disappear. "You would lose the information I have."

"And you would lose your life."

"You wouldn't kill me. I have too much you need."

I turn my eyes on Nash. "Kill hi—"

"No, no. Wait," Daros pleads. "I'll tell you."

"Everything. Now. And it had better be good if you want me to spare you."

"The First Queen—I know how to kill her."

Something flickers in me. "And why would I want to do that?"

"If you haven't noticed yet, you will. There are moments where she wants you to do something you don't want to do. Times you don't feel like yourself. Things about her that make you wonder if she's what she says she is."

My stomach roils with acid. How did he know to voice my quietest fears? And worse—what if he's right, like my gut says he is?

"Why should I believe what you're saying? You've taken everything away from me," I say.

"I have made you what you are," he roars, straining against his chains. "Without me, you'd be nothing. Just another peasant girl, a meal away from starvation."

"I wouldn't have starved. I would have been loved and cherished."

"You would be weak."

I hate it, but he's right.

There's no way I would be queen and able to help Valcora like I want, but then, so many people would be alive, if not for me. Like Queen Deedra. Like Wilric. I pull myself away and back to the task at hand. "How do you know this?"

"Let's just say I have my ways."

"You have given me no reason to trust you, so tell me—how do you know this?"

He sighs, a faint sound. "I realized that the queens started to have patterns over history. They would start out different, but after a time, they would all revert to the same or similar laws and personality. I even found paintings of ones that lived long enough, and in their later years, they started to look alike."

Fear stabs through my chest. "What did they look like?"

"You know, but I'll tell you. They all started with dark, Valcorian hair, but it turned lighter until it was blonde. And no matter what color their eyes were to begin with, they turned a bright green."

My stomach drops far below my bed. Puneah lifts her head to look at me. I can feel Nash's and Jaku's gazes on me as well, but I don't glance at any of them. Just at Daros. If this means what I think it means, the First Queen is trying to replace me so she can rule over my people. And her rule will drown them in misery. "How do I get rid of her?"

My head pounds with the sudden fierceness of the First Queen's presence. It's stronger than I've ever felt it before—a hot anger that's not my own, coursing through me. It's all hers, though I want to howl with her emotion as if it was my own.

"You're feeling her now, aren't you?"

I clench my jaw. "What do I do?"

"First, you're going to get me out of these chains, and then you're going to listen to me and do what I say."

My breathing becomes ragged. I can't trust him, but then, how can I not? If I could move, I'd be punching something. Daros spent my life turning me into exactly what he wanted, and then he used me. And now that I'm finally away from him, I have to fall back in that trap.

To kill the woman trying to take over my life and my country, I must heed the man I despise.

AFTERWORD

If you enjoyed reading this book, please consider helping the
author by leaving a review where you purchased the book and/or
on Goodreads. Even a simple one line review helps.

You can sign up to receive notification when Janeal Falor releases
a new book at www.janealfalor.com with a Release Notification
link on the side bar. Or talk to the author directly at
janealfalor@gmail.com

BOOKS BY JANEAL FALOR

Death's Queen
Death's Queen (Death's Queen #1)
Death's Betrayal (Death's Queen #2)
Death's Embrace (Death's Queen #3)
Death's Assassin (Death's Queen #4)

Mine Series
Mine to Tarnish (Mine Prequel)
You Are Mine (Mine #1)
Mine to Spell (Mine #2)
Mine to Fear (Mine #3)
Sacrifice of Mine (Mine #4)

Darkening Light
Ever Darkening (Darkening Light #1)
Savage Light (Darkening Light #2)

Elven Princess
Bound by Birthright (Elven Princess #1)
Bound to Endure (Elven Princess #2)

Bound by Love (Elven Princess #3)

Standalone
Goddess Ascending
A Genie's Heart

ABOUT THE AUTHOR

Amazon best selling author Janeal Falor lives in Utah with her husband and three children. In her non-writing time she teaches her kids to make silly faces, cooks whatever strikes her fancy, and attempts to cultivate a garden even when half the things she plants die. When it's time for a break she can be found taking a scenic drive with her family or drinking hot chocolate.

www.janealfalor.com
janealfalor@gmail.com